MURDER
AT THE CHERRY FESTIVAL

RICHARD L. BALDWIN

To Jane,
Please enjoy
Rich Baldwin

This novel is a product of the author's imagination. The events described in this story never occurred. Though localities, buildings, and businesses may exist, liberties were taken with their actual location and description. This story has no purpose other than to entertain the reader.

Published by Buttonwood Press
P.O. Box 716
Haslett, Michigan 48840
www.buttonwoodpress.com

—

ISBN: 978-0-9823351-6-1
Printed in the United States of America

I dedicate this book to Hannah Hoffmeister.

Hannah is my eldest granddaughter who at a young age decided to write novels. By the time she was 14 she had written five books in her Dream Ring Series. With assistance from her parents, Amanda and Joe Hoffmeister, and the Buttonwood Press team, her first book, "Ava," was published in 2011. Her second book in the series, "Widdidorm," was published in May of 2012. There are plans to publish the remaining books in her series. Where her writing career will lead is anyone's guess, but for sure, she is a very talented young woman. Needless to say, her maternal grandparents, Nana and myself, are extremely proud of her talent and professionalism, and we commend her for reaching goals most people her age can't imagine.

OTHER BOOKS
BY RICHARD L. BALDWIN

FICTION:

A Lesson Plan for Murder (1998)
ISBN: 0-9660685-0-5. Buttonwood Press.

The Principal Cause of Death (1999)
ISBN: 0-9660685-2-1. Buttonwood Press.

Administration Can Be Murder (2000)
ISBN: 0-9660685-4-8. Buttonwood Press.

Buried Secrets of Bois Blanc: Murder in the Straits of Mackinac (2001)
ISBN: 0-9660685-5-6. Buttonwood Press.

The Marina Murders (2003)
ISBN: 0-9660685-7-2. Buttonwood Press.

A Final Crossing: Murder on the S.S. Badger (2004)
ISBN: 0-9742920-2-8. Buttonwood Press.

Poaching Man and Beast: Murder in the North Woods (2006)
ISBN: 0-9742920-3-6. Buttonwood Press.

The Lighthouse Murders (2007)
ISBN: 978-0-9742920-5-2. Buttonwood Press.

Murder in Thin Air (2008)
ISBN: 978-0-9742920-9-0. Buttonwood Press.

Murder at the Ingham County Fair (2009)
ISBN: 978-0-9823351-0-9. Buttonwood Press.

Murder in Tip-Up Town (2010)
ISBN: 978-0-9823351-2-3. Buttonwood Press.

Assassination at High Speed (2011)
ISBN: 978-0-9823351-4-7. Buttonwood Press.

The Searing Mysteries: Three in One (2001)
ISBN: 0-9660685-6-4. Buttonwood Press.

The Moon Beach Mysteries (2003)
ISBN: 0-9660685-9-9. Buttonwood Press.

The Detective Company (2004; written with Sandie Jones.)
ISBN: 0-9742920-0-1. Buttonwood Press.

SPIRITUAL:

Unity and the Children (2000)
ISBN: 0-9660685-3-X. Buttonwood Press.

NON-FICTION:

The Piano Recital (1999)
ISBN: 0-9660685-1-3. Buttonwood Press.

A Story to Tell: Special Education in Michigan's Upper Peninsula 1902-1975 (1994)
ISBN: 932212-77-8. Lake Superior Press.

Warriors and Special Olympics: The Wertz Warrior Story (2006)
ISBN: 0-9742920-4-4. Buttonwood Press, LLC.

ACKNOWLEDGEMENTS

I wish to thank my editor Anne Ordiway, a gifted master of the English language who works for my readers by giving them an easy to read novel full of interesting characters, twists and turns in plot lines, and allows my writing style and personality to come through the story. Thank you to Joyce Wagner, proofreader, who always picks up some errors in the pre-publication copy. Her eagle eye has saved me in countless previous books. Thank you to Sarah Thomas for once again providing the perfect cover graphics and presenting the text in a most readable format. Thank you to the rest of the Buttonwood Press team for their excellent work: Manager, Vivian Fahle; Bookkeeper, Jennifer Laing; and CPA, Tom Robinson.

I wish to thank Detective David Kirk of the Shiawassee County Sheriff's Department for his advice and input into this novel. Finally, I thank my wife, Patty Moylan Baldwin for her love and support as I follow my dreams.

CHAPTER ONE

Day 1 • July 6

It's the number-one fear of all festival directors—an event that takes full attention from a festival and puts it directly on something unpleasant. It happened to one of the nicest people in the Traverse City area, National Cherry Festival Director, Jerry Waters; he did not deserve the trouble and stress that affected him after a phone call at 8:30 on the morning of July 6th.

"Jerry? This is Police Chief Stacy Bixler. I'm sorry to tell you this, but we have a murder, and it isn't pretty."

"Who? Where? Why?" Jerry asked her in rapid-fire order.

"Your Grand Marshal was shot and likely killed. He's been taken to Munson Medical Center."

"Oh, my God!"

"He was shot by someone around the parade set-up area. The place was full of floats, bands, all kinds of people."

"Was anyone caught?" Jerry asked, hopefully.

"The suspect is a woman, and the answer is, no—the killer is still on the loose. Witnesses said the woman ran from the scene and disappeared in the crowd. Nobody ran after her. People were stunned, running away, and taking cover."

"Oh," Jerry groaned, "this is a nightmare."

"Can you go ahead with the parade?" Stacy asked.

"I've got thousands of people on the parade route, people in the parade from all over Michigan. I can't have a city-wide panic. I'm not sure what to do."

"Just know that whatever you decide, we're there for you. In the meantime, we've an all-points bulletin out in hopes of finding the shooter."

※❀※

The Grand Marshal of the Festival parade was Thomas McNutt, owner of the Northernmost Winery, located on the Old Mission Peninsula. Northernmost Wines were sold throughout the country bringing him fame and fortune. Thomas shared his wealth with Traverse City giving to charities and financing his brainchild, McNutt Horticultural College.

※❀※

Lou Searing, an experienced detective, was walking along the Lake Michigan shore in front of his Grand Haven home when his cell phone rang. Normally beach strolls were his time for meditation and he usually left his phone at the house.

Because Carol was at the exercise club and might need his assistance, he took it along, but when he saw that the caller was not Carol, he pushed "Ignore" and continued to walk.

A former special education administrator-turned-private detective, Lou came by his expertise for solving murders as a result of a motorcycle trip he had taken twelve years ago. He and a buddy had been touring in the eastern part of the country. While camping in the Appalachian Mountains, his friend had been brutally attacked and robbed while sleeping in his tent. The police were slow to act, so Lou set about solving his friend's murder. Since then, he and his partners, first Maggie McMillan, and more recently, Jack Kelly, had built a reputation for assisting law enforcement agencies and solving murders with tireless persistence.

Lou was 70 years old. A childhood case of the measles was responsible for a moderate-to-severe hearing loss. He had male-pattern baldness and was overweight, but his weekly training with a strength coach gave him upper-body firmness. He and his wife Carol enjoyed their adult children, Scott and Amanda, and their spouses Patti and Joe respectively, as well as their eight grandchildren.

To Lou, Carol was simply a beautiful human being. She served on several community boards, her favorite being the Ronald McDonald House. She was a dedicated volunteer, believing that serving this charity was her ministry. She loved gardening, bird-watching, and quilting. And she, in turn enjoyed Lou, who made her laugh every day. The two walked hand-in-hand on the beach every evening when weather permitted.

Lou loved Harley Davidson motorcycles and had ridden them until five years ago when his reaction time slowed and a near-accident convinced him it was time to put the bike in the garage where it leans on its kickstand.

⁂

Jerry had no choice but to proceed with the parade as planned. Of course, word of the shooting in the set-up area traveled along the parade route. The word murder had not been uttered because most believed Thomas had fainted, and a strange "pop" sound had scared a woman who panicked, and that panic spread.

So, right on time, the Cherry Festival Parade began to make its way along the parade route *sans* Thomas McNutt, the Grand Marshal. The terrorism task force of Cherry County went on full alert. Without drawing attention to themselves, SWAT team members suddenly appeared on the roofs of buildings. What most people thought were pleasure aircraft flying a bit low were law enforcement planes seeking anything unfamiliar. More than the usual number of police patrolled the parade route on motorcycles and on foot.

Since it was not an election year, the only politician in the parade was the governor, who attended every year. Why not, when tens and tens of thousands could show their appreciation with waves and applause? This year's governor was newly-elected

Theodore Baker. After the shooting, his guards and aides advised him to drop out, but he would have nothing to do with the suggestion. "I accept the man fainted theory, and a scared woman ran from the scene, period," stated Governor Baker.

"We're in touch with the hospital, Governor, and the man is dead," cautioned security officer Harlan Harris. "He did not faint. A bullet went through his heart."

"Matters not. I came here to be in this parade, and I'm not backing out because a random shooter has killed someone."

"But you'll be out in the open, Governor, an easy target if this killer wants you dead. We can't assure your safety."

"Am I walking or am I riding on the back of a convertible?" Governor Baker asked, seemingly oblivious to the concern for his safety.

"Riding on the convertible, sir."

"Good. It is a long parade."

"Forgive me, sir, but I think you're making a terrible mistake."

"Well, I don't. End of discussion."

"For all we know, the killer is looking for you, too," Trooper Harris replied, thinking this might change the governor's mind.

"That must be my car, the blue one," Governor Baker said paying no attention to Harris. He pointed to a fashionable vehicle. "Good color—goes with my shirt and tie."

⁂

The killer managed to get to the motor home without incident. Before moving on she listened to radio reports of the crisis. The motor home had been stolen two hours earlier at a gas station near Grawn. The driver had left the keys in the ignition when he went into the station to use the restroom and pay for his gas. When he came out, his luxury motor home was gone. There were no witnesses to the theft; people in the area just assumed the person getting behind the wheel was the owner. In fact, the people pumping gas couldn't even recall anyone getting into the motor home.

The thief drove to Traverse City and parked in the library parking lot several blocks from the Cherry Festival parade set-up area. A be-on-the-lookout bulletin was issued once the owner reported the theft, but most of the police in Cherry County were assigned to the festival and other patrols were almost non-existent.

⁂

The ambulance arrived at Munson Medical Center with lights flashing and siren blaring. The driver had alerted the hospital triage staff, "I'm about five minutes out. Victim is a male, approximately 50 years old, vitals are negative. Chest wound, gunshot at close range. Be prepared to find him DOA."

"We'll be ready," replied the triage nurse. "Come on in."

A bay waited to receive the motionless body of Tom Mc-Nutt. A surgery suite was readied should it be needed. It wasn't. There was nothing the hospital staff could do.

⁂

Unknown to anyone, a thirteen-year-old-girl, Sara Laskey, riding her bicycle, heard the pop and saw a woman run. Staying at a distance, she tracked the suspect to the library parking lot and into the motor home. Sara rode home to get her binoculars and digital camera. Then she recorded the license number, took some photos of the motor home, and kept a general eye open for the suspect to exit.

⁂

Lou returned home, washed the sand from his feet and ankles, took his cell phone from his pocket and listened to messages. The first message was a reminder from his Knights of Columbus Council that he had coffee-and-donut duty this Sunday. The second was more official "Lou, this is chief of police Stacy Bixler in Traverse City. Please give me a call. I need your help. Thanks."

Lou dialed the posted number. "Chief, this is Lou Searing. Something's awry at the festival, I presume."

"Yes, sad day up here. The Grand Marshal of our festival parade was murdered an hour ago. We're overwhelmed, as you can imagine. Can you give us a hand?" Chief Bixler asked.

"I'd be happy to," Lou replied. "I'll be right up."

"Thank you. Call me when you get close to Traverse City and I'll send you an escort. Traffic is not moving well. Seems we've got half the state here today."

"Will do. Can you give me any info?" Lou asked.

"Victim is Thomas McNutt. He's a wealthy winery owner and charitable businessman."

"Anything else?" Lou asked.

"He was shot as he sat on the back of a convertible before the parade began. Our suspect is a woman who ran from the scene. Tourists may have photos or a more accurate description before the day is out, but right now information is minimal."

"I'll pack a bag and be on my way. I should arrive within three hours."

"Thanks, Lou."

⚘

Carol Searing arrived home from her workout to find a note on the kitchen counter. "Welcome home. I've gone to Traverse City. Police Chief Bixler has asked me to help her with a murder. Not sure when I'll be home. I'll call. Love you, Lou."

Here we go again, Carol thought. She hated these messages because they meant Lou might be in harm's way. Once again she was put on notice that the peaceful retirement they had planned was in jeopardy. But she loved Lou, and that included his passion for solving murders. All she could do was pray the case could be solved quickly and without harm to anyone.

Carol sat on the porch brushing Samm, the Searing's golden retriever. She lost her appetite for lunch when she read Lou's note. Carol knew Lou was confined to his car so a phone call would not interrupt his work. She called and learned the details of the moment, urged him to be careful, as she always did when he was on a mission, and asked him to call with any news.

As suggested, Lou called Stacy as he passed Interlochen, home of the most famous music academy for youth in the country, if not the world. Chief Bixler asked that he park in a lot at the intersection of M-37 and M-31. A squad car would then take him to Munson Medical Center where he could catch up with Detective Rod Morrison. He would also have the opportunity to speak with Mrs. McNutt.

🎋🌸🎋

Sara Laskey rode by the motor home trying to act like an unsuspecting kid checking out the neighborhood. She noted that all the windows in the motor home were covered with sheet-like material. A second pass by the motor home revealed a Michigan license plate on the vehicle. She intended to make a third pass, but the vehicle suddenly pulled out of the library parking lot.

While her parents watched the parade, Sara had freedom to ride her bike around with friends. Her dilemma was who to go to with the information. She was raised to tell the police if she witnessed a crime but after hours of watching TV crime shows, she had second thoughts. Maybe calling the police was not the best course of action. She was worried about doing the right thing and then becoming either a school hero or the brunt of comments and bullying. She didn't want to be interrogated. She didn't want to look at pages of mug shots. She didn't want to be in a courtroom or questioned by attorneys she didn't know. She decided the safer course of action was to keep what she had seen to herself. She'd watch the newspapers to see if things were resolved without her involvement.

☙❀☙

The weather was perfect for the Cherry Festival Parade. Children got a lot of candy. Governor Baker was happy. But, most important to Jerry Waters the parade went off without a hitch. Rumors swept over the crowd like a dust storm moving over west Texas. People weren't necessarily afraid but they sensed suspense, intrigue, and anxiety. A little kid blew air into his popcorn bag and then popped it. With everyone on edge, the noise set hundreds of hearts beating at a much faster pace than they had seconds before.

The boy's father, sensitive to the situation, picked up the boy and shouted, "Just a paper bag, folks! Sorry for the scare." He led the boy behind the six-deep parade crowd. A policeman approached, thanked the father for reassuring the crowd and shook the boy's hand.

Jerry's phone rang. "Hello," he answered wearily.

"Bet you're relieved," *Traverse City Record Eagle* reporter, Janie Wilks said.

"Well, relieved that the parade is over, but unfortunately, mention of the parade from now on will include the murder of our Grand Marshal," Jerry lamented. "Traverse City has lost a fine man whose wealth has provided many services for needy people."

"I agree. Very sad."

"And you're calling me because?" Jerry asked.

"Because I've been assigned to this story and I would like a comment."

"Well, I already gave you one," Jerry began. "I'm relieved the parade is over and that it went off without a hitch. On the other hand, I'm sorry about the death of Thomas McNutt. He contributed much of his time and money to the community. He'll be missed."

"Did you have any clue such an event would happen today?" Janie asked.

"I trust you, Janie. I haven't told any of this to the police, and I need to give them the info before you share it with the public."

"I understand," Janie replied.

"I didn't take it as a warning at the time, but as I look back, I think I got a subtle message of a threat."

"What was that?" Janie asked.

"A phone call, a woman. At least I *think* it was a woman. She asked about the parade set-up area: where it was, what time set-up would be, and she specifically asked me where the Grand Marshal's vehicle was positioned in the parade."

"I answered her questions. She thanked me and ended with something like, 'I'm sorry to create a headache for you.' Little did I know, huh?"

"Interesting."

"At the time I interpreted 'headache' as simply taking my time to answer three questions. I didn't think she meant a crisis."

"Yeah, it's hard to interpret intent, especially when murder is the last thing on your mind. Let me know when you've talked to the police and whether I can tell my editor the story is a go."

"I will."

꙳❀꙳

As Lou headed to Traverse City, he called his assistant, Jack Kelly. Elaine answered the phone: "Hello, Lou. I know you want Jack, but he had some chores to do at church. Shall I have him call you?"

"Please. I'm on my way to Traverse City."

"Another crime to solve?" Elaine asked.

"Unfortunately, yes."

"Jack will be ready to help you. I suppose this sounds strange, but you know that involving Jack in your work means a great deal to him. You've brought new meaning to his life."

"The benefit is mine. He's an intelligent, deductive thinker. I'm glad he enjoys the work."

"Drive safely, Lou. He'll call you as soon as he gets home. I'd suggest you call him on his cell phone, but it's sitting here on the kitchen counter. He's forgetting this and that with more frequency."

"Welcome to the club."

❀✾❀

The killer drove the motor home into a county park about five miles west of Traverse City where a Chevy pick-up was parked. The suspect took time to make sure nothing was left on the seat and that anything that might have been touched had been wiped free of fingerprints. The vehicle was declared clean as a whistle, with no means of knowing who borrowed it for several hours. She even raked over all footprints in the sandy parking area. There simply was no way to tell who had driven the vehicle.

As she was about to exit the motor home, she opened the glove compartment and took the vehicle's registration. Knowing who owned the vehicle may come in handy.

CHAPTER TWO

Entering the emergency room reception area in Munson Medical Center, Lou saw a variety of patients with summer ailments from sunburn to scraped knees and heat exhaustion. He walked directly to the intake window.

"My name is Lou Searing. I'm here to talk with the police and Mrs. McNutt."

"Yes, Mr. Searing. The police have been expecting you. Come with me." The receptionist led Lou down the hall and into a private room. Mrs. McNutt was sobbing, being comforted by a couple who appeared to be close friends. Lou introduced himself and expressed his sympathies to Mrs. McNutt before inquiring where the detective might be.

"He was called into town," her friend replied, handing another tissue to the distraught widow. "There may be a big break in the case. I think they have captured someone."

"Excuse me. I need to make a call," Lou said, heading into the hall to call Chief Bixler.

"Thanks for being here, Lou," Stacy said.

"No problem. I understand Detective Morrison has gone into town. Is there a lead?"

"I think so. A teenage girl saw the person she thinks may be the killer. I'll let you know what Morrison learns."

Detective Rod Morrison was a 25-year veteran with the Traverse City Police Department. Initially he told Chief Bixler that he resented her bringing Lou into the case. But Chief Bixler convinced Rod that they would be an awesome team. Rod Morrison was a tough, no-nonsense officer. He wore a neatly trimmed beard to hide a two-inch scar, the result of an encounter with a knife-wielding criminal in Lansing, Michigan, where he served 10 years on the police force.

"I'm going to talk with Mrs. McNutt, if she is willing," Lou advised.

"She's a good person," Stacy replied. "We were in a women's club together. Please extend my sympathies and tell her I will see her later."

૪❀૪

Detective Morrison met Sara, her parents, and the family attorney, Ralph Barioto at the Traverse City Police Station. Sara wanted nothing to do with any of it, and even regretted playing Nancy Drew for a few minutes. The situation gave her only bad vibes. She agreed to come forward only after a lecture on good citizenship from her mother.

"Sara, please tell me what you saw," Detective Morrison asked.

Sara looked at the floor, took a deep breath and slowly spoke, "I was on my bike and I heard what I thought was a firecracker. Then I saw a woman walking kinda fast toward the library. A large motor home was in the library lot, about a block from where we live."

"Then, your house is near the parade set-up area?" Officer Morrison asked.

Mrs. Laskey interrupted, "We live about five blocks from the parade set-up area."

Detective Morrison continued. "Sara, can you describe the woman?"

"What do you mean, 'describe'?" Sara asked.

"Was she tall or short, fat or thin, old or young, attractive or plain-looking?"

"I don't know," Sara replied after a few seconds. "She was normal. She looked like my mom, I guess. I really don't remember her face." The detective glanced at Mrs. Laskey and wrote down, "five-foot-four, thin, age forty, brown hair."

"What was she wearing, Sara?"

"Slacks and a T-shirt, I think. Oh, and she was wearing a cap—you know, one of those caps where a pony tail comes out the back."

"Good eye. Did she have a pony tail?" Detective Morrison asked.

"I don't remember."

"How about shoes?"

"I don't know—maybe sandals. I'm not sure."

"Was she carrying anything?"

"A purse. I remember that."

"A handbag or a tote bag? In her hand, or over her shoulder?"

"I think it was a tote bag. As she got close to the mobile home, she pulled keys from the bag."

"Did she look back?" Detective Morrison asked.

"People were running in all directions. She quickly went toward the library and the motor home."

"What about this woman made you suspicious?"

"Well, she didn't open the motor home door when I knocked. Afterward, I thought that was strange."

"You knocked on the door?" Detective Morrison asked, surprised.

"When she was moving fast, something came out of her bag, but she didn't realize it. I picked it up—a cork. I was going to throw it away, but I decided to knock on the motor home door and give it to her. She didn't answer—that's what I thought was odd."

"Do you have this cork?"

"It's in my room at home," Sara replied.

"You didn't tell us about a cork, honey!" her mother said.

"It's just a cork." Sara shrugged her shoulders.

"I'd like to see it, Sara," Detective Morrison said.

"Sure. You can *have* it."

"Good. One of our officers will go to your home and get it. It could be evidence, so please don't touch it. The officer will arrive in an unmarked car so the neighbors won't notice a police car in your driveway."

"Thanks," Sara's father said. "We appreciate that."

"Sara, if you saw a picture of this woman, do you think you could identify her?"

"No. I never saw her face. I just followed her."

"If you think of anything else, please let your parents know, and then give me a call."

"Do you want to see the photos on my digital camera?" Sara asked.

"Certainly. I didn't realize you had taken photos."

"I've read some Nancy Drew books," Sara said with a smile. She showed the photos to Detective Morrison who kept them. In reality they didn't help because the police already had a description of the motor home from when the vehicle was reported stolen.

✖❋✖

Lou found Mrs. McNutt in the chapel of Munson Medical Center. A priest was consoling her. Her head was in her hands and a wadded, damp handkerchief in her lap.

"How is she doing?" Lou asked the priest.

"Better I think. The doctor gave her some medication to calm her."

"Can I ask a few questions, or is this too soon for that?" Lou asked.

"I think she can talk with you. She has been talking with me, and she seems to realize what happened. She is a strong, yet emotional, woman."

Lou approached her, "Mrs. McNutt"

"Yes. Please call me Martha."

"Please accept my sympathy, Martha. I'm very sorry for your loss. Police Chief Bixler asked me to extend her sympathies as well."

"Thank you. Tom was a fine man, such a fine man."

"I'm sure he was," Lou said sympathetically. "My name is Lou Searing. I have been asked by Chief Bixler to help with the investigation. Can I ask a few questions, or would you rather not talk to me now?"

"I simply can't imagine who might have wanted Tom dead. Everybody loved him—or loved his money, is probably a more accurate statement. Our daughter is more upset than I am, if that's possible. She loved her daddy. She always said Tom had more friends than anyone in the world."

"I am sure he was a good man," Lou said sympathetically. "Did he have any enemies in his business, maybe a competitor?"

"Well, competitors come with the business. People who make wine are fully aware of competition."

"Yes, I can imagine. But were any of the competitors nasty, threatening, or unusually confrontational?"

"Tom never mentioned anyone like that. You may want to talk to some of his employees, but my guess is they won't mention anyone."

"Was Mr. McNutt active in a statewide association?" Lou asked.

"Oh, yes, the Wine Growers of Michigan. He was on the board at one time."

"Is there someone I can talk to in that organization?"

"Again, ask his employees, but I expect you'll have a virtual Who's Who of wine-growers in town for his funeral."

"I'm afraid this can't wait that long," Lou responded. "I'll ask his employees. Is there a second-in-command at his business?"

"Yes, Christy. You know, now that you mention it, Christy might have had something to do with his murder."

"Christy?" Lou asked putting his pen to paper.

"Christy Johnson. She's one of those 'can't live with them, can't live without them' types. She made the winery go, but my, what a difficult woman."

"I'll make it a priority to talk with her," Lou said, underlining the name in his small notebook. Following her name, he wrote, *Suspect #1.*

"Please don't tell her I named her as a suspect," Mrs. McNutt said, watching Lou put pen to paper. "That's something I wouldn't want on my plate right now."

"I'll be discreet. I'd also like to talk to your daughter."

"She's under a doctor's care. Her name is Mercy and she's here in the hospital, but you'll need to talk to the medical staff. She's had many mental health issues over the years. I doubt she'll be helpful, but you'll be the judge of that."

"Thank you for your time," Lou said, rising to leave. "Again, I'm sorry for your loss."

⚘

Once Jack returned from his chores, Elaine asked him to call Lou. Jack Kelly was Lou's cohort in solving crimes. He was a retired accountant who had a knack for pulling information together and making sense of data.

"I understand we have a new case," Jack said matter-of-factly. "What can you tell me?"

"I'm up in Traverse City looking into the murder of Thomas McNutt, the Grand Marshal of the Cherry Festival Parade."

"I heard about that on the news," Jack replied.

"I think it will be challenging. In my opinion it has nothing to do with the Cherry Festival and everything to do with some sort of revenge."

"Doesn't every murder?" Jack asked.

"I suppose so, to some extent."

"Do you need me in Traverse City?" Jack asked.

"Actually, I need you to become a winery expert."

"Expert, as in tasting?" Jack wondered. "You know I don't enjoy the taste of alcohol in any form."

"No, not tasting, but in the business of running a winery. You might want to go to the Paw Paw area in the southwest part of the state," Lou suggested. "There are several growers there who could help you learn the ins and outs of the business."

"OK. I have got my marching orders. Be in touch."

⚘

While Lou was on his way to The Northernmost Winery to talk with Christy he gave much thought to the murder itself. *Why would someone commit a murder in broad daylight with hundreds of people around? It made no sense. A parade of any size usually begins with a police car or motorcycle officers leading the way and keeping the parade-goers close to the curb. Sirens and flashing lights get people excited. Any number of people could witness a shooting, even one with a silencer on the firearm. So, in planning this murder, why would a killer boldly commit the crime in daylight with police in the vicinity and hundreds of potential witnesses? Unless, that is, he or she wanted to be caught.*

⋊❀⋉

The cork taken from the Laskey home was sent to the State Police Crime Laboratory for analysis. It was only a cork, and without something to identify where it was used or manufactured, it would likely be of little help. But it had been touched, and the mostly smooth surface might display a fingerprint.

Jack began his research with Google. He entered "Cork" in the search engine and brought up enough material to occupy his mind for a couple of days. After perusing more than he wanted to know about cork he entered "wine-making" into the search window. Once again, a treasure trove of information came onto his screen. He chose www.winemakermag.com, and within a few seconds all he needed to know to make wine was on the computer screen. With a hot cup of coffee beside him, Jack began an introductory course in operating a winery.

⋊❀⋉

The killer was certain she had committed the perfect crime. She had stolen the vehicle, shot McNutt, gotten out of town, left the motor home in an empty county park, and now waited in a cabin on Sanford Lake, a bit south of Lake Ann, a small community between Traverse City and the shore of Lake Michigan. She opened the refrigerator, took out a cold Diet Vernor's, and collapsed into an easy chair. The day had been tiring and stressful. She simply wanted to relax, take a few deep breaths, close her eyes, and drift off to sleep, leaving the soda to go warm and lose its flavor.

When she awoke she turned on the television to see any reports of the murder, but there were none. She retrieved her wallet from her tote. At the same time, she remembered the cork she had picked up at the Northernmost Winery early that morning. She took it thinking she could somehow implicate the cork salesman in the death of Tom. She had been sure it was in her tote bag. She went out to her truck to check on the seat and on the floor, but the cork was not there, either.

⚘

Lou called the Northernmost Winery and asked to speak to Christy, but she was not available. Just about everyone was taking in the activities offered by the world-famous Cherry Festival in Michigan's paradise of a vacation land. Lou left a message on Christy's extension, "This is Lou Searing, I'm assisting in the investigation of Thomas McNutt's murder. Please call at your earliest convenience." Lou left his cell phone number.

Within a minute his phone vibrated. The display read, C. Johnson. *That didn't take long,* Lou thought.

"Hello."

"Mr. Searing. This is Christy Johnson. You called?"

"Yes. Thank you for a quick return call."

"Not a problem. Calls have been coming in from all over the country. I feel like a human switchboard."

"I can imagine. Mrs. McNutt indicated that you were Tom's right-hand person. I'm hoping you can shed some light on this tragedy."

"We're in a state of shock around here. Nobody can believe this would happen to Mr. McNutt. The guy didn't have any enemies. He was loved, respected, and a pillar of the community. And I might add, a stalwart member of the wine-making family."

"As far as the winery goes, can you think of anyone who might have a grudge or may have had an encounter with Thomas?" Lou asked.

"Other than myself, I can't think of…"

"Other than yourself?" Lou asked, surprised.

Christy hesitated. "You can't run a winery without knocking heads with the boss from time to time. Of course, we didn't always see eye-to-eye on many aspects of the operation. Some of the staff here would probably tell you that I couldn't be happier about his murder. A few may even tell you I killed him, or at a minimum, paid to have him killed."

"I've interviewed many people in my investigating, but no one has ever admitted to being a suspect."

"Can't deny reality."

"Well then, *did* you kill him or arrange for his death?"

"Now, Mr. Searing, let's get real here," Christy replied with disgust. "Biting the hand that feeds me is not common sense. I did not kill Tom McNutt!"

"You can't blame me for asking. After all, you said you could be a suspect."

"I understand. Do you want to come to the winery? You're certainly welcome. I'm expecting the police soon. They will undoubtedly be looking for clues."

"That's their job," Lou replied. "I'll leave that work to them. But, yes, I would like to come to the winery, and maybe you could give me a tour."

"I'd be glad to. Tell me when you'll arrive, and I'll give you a tour—answer any questions you have."

"Thank you. I have a few other higher priorities at the moment, but I'll call and make arrangements."

✿❀✿

Jack was up to his virtual ears in wine corks. He found the subject fascinating; he'd had no idea how and where corks were made, or what happened to them after the wine bottle was opened. He discovered that most corks are made in Portugal and Spain. They could be sold either plain or stamped with designations of the winery.

⚘

Lou wanted to talk to Jerry Waters, the Cherry Festival Director. This was a hectic and stressful day for Jerry, but Lou had a murder to solve and questions which couldn't wait.

Lou found Jerry in the Festival Headquarters on Sixth Street. Reporters, police, volunteers, and board members crowded into his office. Each had a mission, whether it was offering information, asking for directions, or simply wanting to be where the action was.

Lou stopped at the office door and got Jerry's attention. Jerry stopped what he was doing and walked directly to Lou, shook his hand, and said, "Boy, am I glad to see you!"

"I would have liked to have seen you in less stressful times, but I guess we play the cards dealt to us, right?"

"Yes, and, I just got a useless hand," Jerry replied, shaking his head.

"I know you're busy, but I wanted to let you know I was in town and on the case. I've talked to Mrs. McNutt and to Christy Johnson at the winery. And Jack is learning everything he can about corks."

"That's the Lou I know—already deep into the mystery. What do you need at the moment?" Jerry asked.

"I am wondering if before the parade set-up was underway, you were visited or got a phone call that was out of the ordinary."

"The morning of the parade is pure chaos. No matter how much pre-planning goes into such an event, there are issues to be addressed. But, I did get a call. A woman asked about the set-up area and a question about the Grand Marshal's vehicle or place in the parade."

"Interesting. You obviously don't keep all calls in a log or audio-record them?"

"No. It was just one of many."

"How did she get through?" Lou asked. "Don't you have a receptionist who screens calls? I mean, on parade day, you must be as busy as a bee."

"I hadn't thought about that. Gayle, my secretary usually answers all calls, but I didn't think to ask her why she let a call through to me when she knew all the answers. Hmmm, good question, Lou."

"Is Gayle here?" Lou asked.

"Yes. She's the tall woman over by the door, talking to the reporter wearing a red baseball cap."

"I'll check with her. Before I go, let me ask, could there a connection between his being murdered and his being Grand Marshal of your parade?"

"I haven't had time to think about it," Jerry replied looking puzzled. "Tom was chosen as Grand Marshal by our Festival Board, who reviewed many applications."

"So, others were being considered?" Lou asked.

"Certainly. This is a prestigious honor. A lot of status comes with the designation."

"I'd like a list of those who were considered, along with support letters or minutes of meetings where Grand Marshal candidates were discussed."

"Gayle can get that for you. She was my representative at every committee meeting."

"OK. I know we'll talk again as the investigation continues, but for now, who was the driver of the Grand Marshal vehicle?"

"Eric Williams. He's the owner of the largest cherry-growing farm in this region."

"And, I'll bet my life savings that he was one of those up for Grand Marshal," Lou predicted.

"Yes, as a matter of fact he was."

"Get back to your busy day, Jerry. I'll talk to Gayle and then head up to the winery to see Christy."

"Thanks for being here, Lou. I feel better knowing you're helping with the investigation."

Gayle had just finished her conversation with the reporter as Lou approached.

"Excuse me, Gayle?"

"Yes."

"I'm Lou Searing. I'm helping the police investigate the murder. May I ask you a few questions?"

"I am very busy as you can imagine. How about tomorrow?"

"I'd rather ask my questions now," Lou countered.

"Well, I'd rather answer them tomorrow," Gayle replied, obviously not wanting to be bothered. "I'm swamped by all of this confusion."

"I can appreciate that, but I need information you might have. You had time for that reporter, but you don't have time for me?"

"That's right. Excuse me," Gayle said as she moved to her right, leaving Lou standing alone.

This was neither the time nor the place for a scene. Lou would get answers to his questions eventually. However, this exchange left a bitter taste in Lou's mouth and evoked the thought that Gayle might be involved in the crime.

✿✻✿

Almost immediately, the festival resumed its busy pace. The weather was perfect, and thousands of tourists were enjoying midway rides, the craft show, the cherry pit-spitting contest, and a host of other events. The murder was a black mark on the day, but people were in Traverse City for fun and the crime, while horrific, quickly left their minds at Michigan's favorite summer festival.

✿✻✿

Jack needed a break from corks. He drove from Muskegon into southwest Michigan, looking for a winery far from the action in Traverse City. When he reached Paw Paw's Hilltop Winery, he went into the wine-tasting and gift shop.

"Can I interest you in some of our wine?" the sales representative asked.

"No thanks, but perhaps you can help me. I'd like to talk to someone who knows about running a winery."

"Are you thinking of owning a winery?" she asked.

Jack laughed. "No, no. I'm a criminal investigator. I work with Lou Searing, looking into crimes in Michigan."

"You think we're involved in the murder of Mr. McNutt?" the representative asked, surprised.

"Absolutely not. But, we need some basic information about how a winery is run," Jack responded. "You know about his murder?"

"News travels fast in the winery community. We're like family."

"Well, I'm sorry for your loss. Is there someone who could help me?"

"I'll see if Jim is available. If anyone comes in, please tell them I'll be back shortly."

"Thank you."

Within a couple of minutes a short, stocky man sporting a goatee and wearing a fashionable suit and shined shoes appeared. "Mr. Kelly?"

"Yes."

"I'm, Jim Rashid. I understand you have some questions about how a winery operates."

"Yes. As I mentioned to your staff member, I'm working with Lou Searing, investigating the McNutt murder in Traverse City. Part of the investigation involves corks and how a winery operates. It appeared to me that your winery is quite large, so I thought I'd see how grapes become wine."

"I'd be glad to help. I think the best way to help you understand our operation is to give you a tour. Let's go to the vineyard."

After a short tour of the vineyard and the wine-making process, Jim brought up the murder of Thomas McNutt, his friend and colleague. "I think you're wasting energy looking into winery operations."

"We have reason to believe the killer is connected to the wine industry," Jack replied.

"I don't know what information you have, but I know this business and the people in it. No one, absolutely no one, would kill Tom McNutt."

"A competitor couldn't be jealous of his success?" Jack reasoned.

"We're all jealous of his success, but when Tom succeeds, we all succeed. Wine consumption is up, and in spite of the economy, all of us are selling more wine."

"Can you suggest a motive for the killer?" Jack asked.

"No, except to say that when you find him or her, the killer won't have a connection to his winery or to any other winery."

"You may be right."

Jim seemed to grow impatient with Jack's questions, giving hints that he had overstayed his welcome. Jack realized he only had time for a couple more questions.

"I appreciate your help, Jim. I'm sure you have plenty of work to do and I need to be on my way, but just a couple more questions." Jim took a deep breath and gave a slight nod.

"Are the grapes grown in your vineyards the only grapes in your wine?"

Jim was taken aback by Jack's question. After a short pause he responded, "For the most part the answer is yes. But we do import some grapes from Missouri and Wisconsin."

"I assume that's legal?"

"Yes, it is."

"Then why does your label read, 'Michigan Wine from Michigan-Grown Grapes'? Isn't that a violation of the 2006 Wine Trade Agreement? It's my understanding that to claim wine from a specific winery, all the grapes need to be grown there."

"Listen, you're out of my league," Jim responded, obviously perturbed. "If you want to know how to make wine, come to me. If you have legal questions, see a lawyer. Excuse me. I've given you far more time than I normally give our guests."

"Thank you, Mr. Rashid. I have an appreciation of a Michigan industry and a respect for each of you. Thanks for talking with me."

❊❊❊

While sitting in his car in the winery parking lot, Jack called Lou. "I touched a nerve in Paw Paw, Lou."

"It isn't the first time and won't be the last," Lou replied.

"I was talking to a winery owner near Paw Paw. Prior to my visit, I read on the Internet about a Wine Trade Agreement and knew it was illegal to claim a wine was produced by a grower unless all the grapes came from the grower's vineyards. I asked a simple question about where his grapes came from."

"So, you set him up, is that what you're saying?" Lou asked.

"I guess so, but I didn't intend to begin World War III."

"Looks like either it's a common practice, or we're opening Pandora's box to find grapes from all over the world," Lou said.

When Lou heard of Jim's belief that the killer would have no connection to the wine industry, he replied, "He may have a point. Tom could be involved in a love triangle or some ugly activities in the skeleton closet, like gambling or drugs. We're all shocked when we discover a leader in the community makes bad decisions and gets into messy situations."

"Happens more often than we think," Jack replied.

"Listen, Jack. I'm going to pull you off cork-and-wine detail and ask you to wait for a new assignment."

"My pleasure to serve, Lou. What can I do?"

"I am heading out to Tom's winery and I suspect I'll have something for you to work on. Stay tuned."

"I look forward to hearing from you."

❀❋❀

After talking to Jack, Lou called Christy and learned that she would be available in about an hour. Lou drove along Old Mission Road enjoying the scenery and stopping at an occasional stand for some fresh fruit. He eventually arrived at the Northernmost Winery sign and drove down a dirt road until he came to a mansion surrounded by fields of grapes and cherries stretching as far as he could see.

A woman standing in the parking lot seemed to be waiting for him. She approached Lou as he got out of his car. "Welcome to our winery. I assume you're Mr. Searing."

"Yes, I am. You must be Christy," Lou stated. Christy was dressed in professional summer attire. She was fairly tall, slim, and attractive. Her hair color was dark brown and was cut short.

"Yes. I came out here because with so many people around, I thought we either should have a private conversation outside or take a ride in your car."

"That's an idea," Lou replied. "Let's go for a ride."

As Lou and Christy pulled on to the Old Mission Road, Lou remarked, "I'm looking for a motive and possible suspects.

On the phone you suggested yourself, but then took me to task when I asked if you were involved."

"I was serious, but I didn't expect you to take me at my word."

"I listen carefully to everything I hear related to a crime. Information comes in many forms and I take nothing lightly nor dismiss anything off-hand."

"Well, let me set the record straight. I did not kill Tom McNutt."

"Okay, that's on the record. Who *did kill* him?" Lou asked. "Any thoughts?"

"No one comes to mind."

"Bring me into his life, Christy."

"Meaning?"

"Meaning, tell me about the man. I know he owned this winery, but that's about all. What were his hobbies, passions?" Lou asked.

"Oh, I see. He invested a lot of his time, energy, and money in the college named after him."

"Oh, yes. That's a plant science specialty school, correct?"

"Yes. Students from around the world enroll there. Wine-making is a huge draw, but a lot of their research is funded by the federal government."

"So, in that world, is there anyone who would want Tom killed? You know, a disgruntled student, a fired professor, a student who failed a class?"

"I really have little knowledge of that part of his life. He never said much about the place to me."

"Okay. Let's move on. Was he a gambler?" Lou asked.

"Yes, he was always betting on sports events. He had a bookie in Vegas who advised him and was his representative on the gambling scene. Actually, he and I were both into gambling. His was big-time and I was small-time." Christy and Lou chuckled.

"Any other skeletons in the closet?" Lou asked. "A mistress, drug use, excessive drinking?"

"I never saw the closet. One reason he was such a successful man was his self-control. He seemed to be a clean-cut man. Now, that doesn't mean there were no skeletons, but I'd be very surprised to hear of any."

"Other than gambling, you mean?" Lou reminded Christy.

"I stand corrected."

"Did he have any expensive hobbies?"

"Only one that I know of."

"And that would be?"

"Ocean sailing. Not many knew that he was a skipper in big races, like America's Cup. He had a crew of five young men who worked for him. Other than grapes, that was his passion."

"Did he compete in the Chicago-to-Mackinac or Port Huron-to-Mackinac races?"

"I think so. I never heard about that part of his life either. As far as I know, his crew and captain handled all aspects of the competition. He would fly in his corporate jet to Sydney, for example, for a race. It almost seemed like a business trip."

"Was he active in politics?" Lou asked.

"No, he had no interest in politics. I think he contributed to a few campaigns, but as far as running for office or advising elected officials, that was not his cup of tea. He saw that world as corrupt at best, and therefore he put no energy into it."

"Individual sports?"

"You mean like golf, tennis, that sort of thing?" Christy asked.

"Yes."

"Lousy golfer, and as far as I know, he never touched a tennis racket in his life. He was a warm-weather guy, so skiing was out."

"Okay. You've been very helpful. Let's go back to the winery." Lou continued his questions. "Might a competitor or business associate have been jealous of Tom's success or want Tom dead for any reason?"

"I'd tell you if I knew of anyone, but nobody comes to mind. He ran a tight ship here."

"He only used these grapes in his wines, I assume?" Lou said after looking over an expanse of vineyards.

Christy paused. Lou glanced at Christy, his eyebrows raised. "Your silence tells me the answer is no."

"We do import some grapes here."

"Europe?" Lou asked.

"No, mainly from California."

"I assume this is legal?"

"I've never thought about it. I don't think Tom would knowingly break any law."

"That big sign near your entrance reads, *Michigan wine, made from choice Michigan grapes.* So, it appears that isn't entirely true."

Again, a telling pause. "I really need to get back to the office and handle the calls that are coming in. I'm sure you understand."

On the way back, Lou asked about McNutt's family. "He was married, correct?" Lou asked, although he knew the answer.

"Twice married. He was married to Joanne—I liked Joanne. We really hit it off. The four of us did a lot of social events together."

"By four you mean??

"I mean Tom, Joanne, my husband Gerry, and me."

"So, you four attended a number of high society events?"

"I wouldn't say high society here in Traverse City, but yes, we would go together. Tom would almost always be one of the huge contributors and of course he could bring whomever he wished. Most of the time, a good friend and I went with them."

Lou continued his questions. "I take it there was a divorce?"

"I'd call it a life-long separation. It was ugly."

"Tom had a mistress?"

"It was complicated and messy. Tom didn't want it to be out in public. He just put her out of his life and moved on."

"Put her out of his life?" Lou asked.

"Just moved on. I can't say it any better. He seemed to wake up one morning and resumed life as a bachelor."

"He paid her to be quiet?"

"He didn't pay her, he just ended it."

"You can't just end it. There are legal papers and settlements."

"Not when you are Tom McNutt."

"So, then Martha came along?" Lou asked.

"Yes. I don't know much about her. You see, after the separation from Joanne, to this day, the social events stopped. I only saw Martha a few times, and the vibes weren't there. She wasn't my type. So, since Martha, I'm not helpful."

"Tom and Joanne had a daughter?" Lou asked, again knowing the answer but hoping Christy would add something."

"Yes, and she was mentally ill almost from the time she was born. This brought a lot of stress to Tom. Mercy is her name; she was going to be the perfect daughter and the apple of Tom's eye. But it was soon obvious that she had problems that couldn't be overcome with the resources here in Traverse City."

"Well, here we are," Lou said, approaching the winery. "You've been very helpful, Christy. Thank you for talking with me."

"You're welcome. Do the police have a suspect?"

"No. A woman was seen hurrying to the library parking lot and getting into a motor home. A teenage girl saw her and has been talking to the police. But, that's all we have so far."

"Well, I certainly hope you find the killer. Terrible tragedy."

The two bid farewell with the expectation that they would talk again. Christy promised her cooperation in the investigation. She got out of Lou's car and walked toward the winery office.

Like the famous television detective, Colombo, Lou called to Christy, "One more question, please."

Christy turned and looked back. "Yes?"

"Was Tom active in a church?"

"Talk to Father Pat at St. Joe's in town." She turned and walked into the winery.

Before driving into town, Lou called Jack. "I need you to look into Tom McNutt's involvement in ocean and Great Lakes sailboat racing. He competed in the America's Cup race and other races around the world. He also entered races to Mackinac Island. See if you can find any sinister activity; a suspect may surface. I still think there is a connection to the wine industry. I would like you to look into possible illegal activity or shady practices that Tom McNutt might have been involved in."

"I'll get right on it. Do you need me in Traverse City?"

"Not yet. In fact I'll probably go home tomorrow. I can get only so much preliminary information. My gut tells me we'll be on this case for some time."

⚘

When the sun had almost set, a lone fisherman in a rowboat eased a heavy duffel bag into Sanford Lake and watched it sink. The bag held a .38 magnum pistol with a silencer, a pony-tail wig, a baseball cap, slacks, shirt, surgical gloves, a tote bag, socks, sandals, and a heavy rock. The bag sank to the bottom of the lake, and in that instant, the fisherman was confident that evidence for the crime wouldn't be found.

CHAPTER THREE

Since not a single motel room was available in Traverse City or anywhere in the area because of the festival, Lou decided to head back to Grand Haven. He had gathered a lot of information in a short time, but he decided to stop at St. Joe's church to talk with Father Pat. The chances of finding him were slim, but nothing ventured, nothing gained. He set his GPS for the church and followed the directions to the front door.

Lou looked at the sign in front of the church, glanced at his watch and realized that he had arrived during confessions. He thought, *Maybe he could catch Father at the end of confessions, or if nobody was confessing today, perhaps Father was in his office.*

Lou entered the church and walked to the office. The sign on that door read, "I am hearing confessions. If you need to see me for any other reason, please wait in a pew outside the confessional."

Lou opened the door to the sanctuary and saw the confessional near the back left. Father Pat's name was over one door, and both doors were closed, so Lou took a seat in a pew.

The silence offered a restful escape from the noise of the festival and the scurrying of thousands of people. Lou found himself in prayer, asking for guidance in solving this injustice. He was in the middle of the Lord's Prayer when he heard the door open, and out stepped Mrs. McNutt.

Lou rose. "Mrs. McNutt. We meet again."

"Yes. I wanted to talk to Father Pat about Tom's funeral service. But, why would *you* be outside a confessional at St. Joe's?" Martha McNutt asked.

"It's a fair question, and let's just say that investigating a crime takes me to a whole lot of people and places. At the moment, I need to talk with Father Pat."

"So, this has to do with Tom?" Martha asked.

"That would be a safe assumption."

"I don't think Father can divulge any information about the annulment. I assume that's what you want to know."

"I appreciate your curiosity about my visit with Father, but confidentially is important in my line of work."

"Yes, of course. Have a good day Mr. Searing."

"Thank you, Martha." Mrs. McNutt nodded in Lou's direction and walked out of the sanctuary.

Father Pat emerged from his side of the confessional. "Are you here for confession or to see me?" he asked.

"Just a minute of your time, Father."

"How can I help you?"

"My name is Lou Searing. I'm working with the police, investigating the death of Tom McNutt. During an earlier interview, I asked about Tom's religion, and someone suggested I talk with you. Can you tell me anything that might help me understand his death?"

"Tom was the answer to every priest's prayers. Whenever I needed money, I would call Tom, and after I described the church's need, he would open his wallet and offer more than I asked."

"I imagine you would find him a great resource."

"You asked whether there is anything that might help you understand his death. My answer is, yes."

Lou took out his notebook and a pen.

"Tom was not a member of the Catholic church. His parents were Dutch Reformed, raising Tom in the traditions of their faith. But Tom's aunt and uncle McNutt were Catholic and made Tom feel welcome in their church."

"So he went to the Catholic church, but was not a member?"

"That's right."

"But, not being a member, he could not receive the sacraments, correct, Father?"

"That's correct."

"Mrs. McNutt seems to be holding up pretty well," Lou said. "Odd that on the day of his murder his wife is in the church seeking forgiveness for sins."

Father Pat looked puzzled, then his face cleared. "Martha McNutt comes to confession every week, no matter what is going on around her. I can understand your thought, but I'm not surprised, and if you knew Martha, you would understand."

"Interesting. She told me you wouldn't be able to tell me anything about the annulment."

"She's right."

"Her remark came right out of nowhere, Father. I didn't know anything about an annulment."

"It's best nothing more be said."

"Can you tell me about Tom's daughter?"

"Very sad. She has serious mental health issues, and she's getting the best care money can buy, but nothing works: drugs; therapy. She's sedated to keep her behavior under control."

"So, I won't be able to interview her?" Lou asked.

"You could probably interview her, but little she said would make sense. She has no idea who her mother or father is, where she is, or anything in reality."

"I see. I began this conversation by asking if you knew anything that would explain the murder of Tom McNutt.

You replied that he was not Catholic. Were you just relaying a fact or do you think that has something to do with his murder?"

"Just stating information about him. No, I don't think his religious standing has anything to do with his death."

"Okay, then let me finish by asking if you know anything that *would* explain Tom's death."

For a telling moment, Father Pat seemed deep in thought. Finally, he looked Lou in the eye and calmly said, "Trouble followed Tom McNutt. His money has always been able to make the trouble *de jour* go away or subside."

"Interesting. What kind of trouble?" Lou asked.

"For now, I would rather not comment."

"'I respect that, Father. Thank you for talking with me." The two shook hands. Lou walked to his car and began the long trip back to Grand Haven.

❧ ❀ ❧

As Lou drove down US 31 South, he called Detective Rod Morrison. The Traverse City police still had little information. They had the bullet, but without the firearm, it was useless. But people interviewed at the scene agreed they saw a woman with a pony tail in the vicinity of the Grand Marshal's car, and their descriptions matched Sara's.

The float driver, Eric Williams, was no help. He had been facing forward and said he didn't even realize that Tom had been shot. He had wondered why everyone scattered, but he didn't realize that Tom had fallen to his right and tumbled onto the pavement until several seconds after he was shot.

One witness who came forward provided a memory of the minute before the shooting. He was watching the woman suspect and noticed that she approached the Grand Marshal's vehicle, actually talking with the driver for several seconds. He assumed they were friends. He wasn't looking in that direction when the commotion began, but he wanted police to know that the suspect did seem to know the driver before a gun was fired.

Detective Morrison had asked if there was any interaction between the woman and Mr. McNutt: the answer was no. The witness stated that he only recalled seeing Mr. McNutt get up on the back of the convertible. He did recall, however, that a photographer took pictures of Tom seated on the vehicle. The witness thought the man likely had been a newspaper photographer.

※❀※

The cork that Sara saw fall out of the suspect's tote bag was sent to the State Police Crime Laboratory in Grayling, Michigan, for analysis. Preliminary results showed that the cork had been used in a wine bottle. The engraving on the cork was difficult to discern, but with high-tech scanning devices, the lab technician was fairly certain they could find the name of the winery. An analysis was done for fingerprints or DNA, but those results were not available yet.

꒰❋꒱

When Jack went to the Internet to find out about Tom's ocean sailing events, he found more than he needed to know about the sport. Jack entered "Thomas McNutt" in the search engine for one of the most popular sites and was surprised to see results of various races.

Tom's craft usually finished in the lower half of the competition. There was a photo of Tom and his craft, crew and captain. The sailing vessel was huge, and the crew was a good-looking group of college-aged men. The captain was a man in his forties identified in the caption as Warren Lofts of the San Francisco Bay Sailing Club. Jack looked up Warren and learned that he had captained other boats. Whenever he captained a sailing craft in competition he seemed to either win or come in second. He was always in the money.

This seemed odd. Perhaps the quality of Tom's yacht was inferior. What other conclusion could be drawn? However, when Tom and Warren co-captained the ship, the results were pathetic. A lot of money is lost when a ship doesn't finish in the money. Jack made a note to contact Mr. Lofts.

Given San Francisco was three time zones away, Jack took a chance that Warren would be ashore at the yacht club. It was Jack's lucky day, because Warren was in the bar and took the call.

"Mr. Lofts?"

"Yes. Who's calling?"

"This is Jack Kelly, calling from Michigan. I'm investigating the murder of Thomas McNutt. You know of the murder, I assume?"

"Yeah, very sad. Tom was a nice guy. Mrs. McNutt called me very soon after the tragedy. She knew I would want to know."

"I see."

"Why are you calling me?"

"We need to know as much about the victim as possible, and I learned he was into ocean sail racing. I saw your photo with the crew on the Internet and thought you might know who might have wanted him dead, or you might give me a lead about what to look into."

"Makes sense. Well, let's see. Who might have wanted him killed?" Warren repeated. A few seconds later he replied, "No one immediately comes to mind."

"When you two were together, did he ever express concern about a disagreement with someone, or say that working with someone was stressful?"

"I recall frustration with Christy at the winery. He saw her as a dominant, pushy female. Those were his exact words, repeated often enough for me to remember them."

"I've taken note of Christy. Was any other person or circumstance a burr under his saddle?"

"He was a pretty easy-going guy—not much got to him. Christy is the only one who seemed to be as you say, 'a burr under his saddle.'"

"Thanks for talking with me. None of my business, but what happens to you and your crew now that Tom has died?"

"At the moment, I'm trying not to think about it. We had language written into our wills and estate plans that transferred ownership of the yacht to the other in the event that either of us died. So, I anticipate some legal procedures, and then I'll assume full ownership of the Cherry Princess."

"Will you fly to Traverse City for his funeral?"

"No. I don't know the family or mutual friends. Besides, I have a race in Australia in a few days, and I think Tom would want me on the water, enjoying memories of our racing."

"Thanks for talking with me, Mr. Lofts."

"My pleasure. Good luck with your investigation."

⚘

It was approaching midnight when Lou pulled into his driveway, but Carol was still up. The half-moon was bright over a calm Lake Michigan.

"You've had a long day, Lou. Want to take a short walk on the shore or simply hit the hay?" Carol asked.

"Actually, a walk would be great. Yes, it's been a long day, but adrenaline is still coursing the veins and I need time with you, and the water lapping over my feet and ankles to relax."

The two walked hand-in-hand to the water's edge and headed south along the shore. The temperature was a perfect 68 degrees, the moon flickered brightly off the water, and the peace was welcome.

"You'll probably not want to talk about this case, but if you do, I'm here to listen," Carol said lovingly.

"I've a feeling this is going to be a tough one."

"How so?"

"People are saying this guy didn't have an enemy in the world, everyone loves the guy or his money. Well, even a guy worth billions has enemies. Money does that—opens doors, but it also allows in a lot of strange characters. Supposedly there are no skeletons in this guy's closet, but once again, everybody has one, if not more."

"In other words, there could have been several reasons to kill him," Carol reasoned.

"Right, but two questions stick in my mind."

"They are?" Carol asked.

"Why was he shot in such an open area? It was daylight, and people were milling around. The chance of being seen, wrestled to the ground, or confronted by a police officer were high. Secondly, what was so important about killing him in the parade set-up area?"

"Yes, that is odd."

"And then I stopped at a Catholic church to see a Father Pat, who was supposed to have pertinent details about his religion. I happened to stop during confession time, and as I sat in the pew waiting, out of the confessional stepped Mrs. McNutt. She greeted me and said, 'Father won't be able to tell you anything about the annulment.' Why would she lead with that? No annulment had come to my attention previously. This may be a significant factor that just jumped out at me."

"Sounds like a successful first day," Carol concluded. "Is Jack helping you?"

"I didn't ask him to come to Traverse City. Another car in town was the last thing the place needed. I mean, I can't recall so many people in one town in my life. I asked him to research corks..."

"Corks?" Carol interrupted.

"A cork fell out of the suspect's tote bag when she got her keys out to open the stolen motor home. I asked Jack to become an expert in wine bottle corks. And, I found out that Mr. McNutt was into ocean sailing, so Jack is now looking into that world." Thoroughly confused, Carol decided not to ask anything more.

Lou and Carol stopped at their favorite large piece of driftwood, one that seemed to have two hollowed-out seats made just for them. Still holding hands, they looked over a calm and serene Lake Michigan under a bright moon, took deep breaths, and enjoyed being together.

CHAPTER FOUR

Day 2 • July 7

The killer awoke to a steady rain. There was no reason to get up, since her daring mission had been skillfully accomplished. As far as she knew, there were no witnesses to the theft of the motor home, and nobody saw the crime take place. But there was the girl who knocked on the motor home's door for no reason she could fathom. She had carefully pulled aside the sheet covering the window and saw the girl get on her bike and ride toward the parade area.

The killer couldn't get back to sleep; she could only toss and turn, thinking about the girl in Traverse City. *The kid could have the cork. She could have seen her outfit and may even be able to identify her.* As she lay on the cabin's cot, she couldn't help thinking that this girl was a threat to her perfect crime.

❀

Sara got exactly what she feared. She hadn't wanted to be the center of attention, and she had not wanted to go to the authorities. But, she had and now she was angrier at her mother than before.

"I *knew* this was going to happen!" Sara shouted.

"*What* was going to happen?" her mother asked.

"I'm being called names and being made fun of by my friends, and it's all because you made me go to the police."

"It was the right thing to do, Sara."

"Maybe to your way of thinking, but it doesn't *feel* like you're protecting me. I'm in the newspaper and on television. I can't go anywhere without someone calling me 'Little Miss Nancy Drew' and laughing, or making remarks like, 'Seen a good killing lately?'"

"Sara Laskey! No one is saying that to you! I can't believe it."

"Well, it's true. I'm embarrassed and humiliated! I knew it would be this way!" Sara burst into tears.

"I'm sorry, Sara, but good citizens report what they see."

"I hate this! And now I'll have to go to court and then I'll have to be afraid that woman will want revenge for what I did to her. I just want to disappear! I hate this!"

"Disappear? Where would you go?" her mom asked.

"I'm not sure—somewhere where people don't know who I am or what I've seen."

"Sara Laskey, you are not going anywhere," Mrs. Laskey affirmed. "You are much too young, and you know your father and I would worry ourselves sick if you weren't with us."

"If you find a note and I'm gone, that's just the way it is. I don't want to keep on living like this!" Sara ran to her room and slammed the door.

Mrs. Laskey felt sorry for Sara. She was a sensitive young girl, but she was also rebellious and had threatened to run away in the past. She thought, *Maybe I shouldn't have made a big deal out of this. Too late now, though. I've got to help her through this.*

Sara called her best friend, Sandy. She had demonstrated immaturity in the past, but today Sandy was surprisingly logical. "I know how you feel, but your mom is right. Talking to the police was the right thing to do. And, yes, the attention is on you now, but in a few more days, you'll be old news. Don't do anything stupid in the meantime."

"I've got to get out of here. There's a vacant cabin next to ours. The owner gave Mom the key in case she needed to get in or let someone in. If I can get to our cabin, I would have a place to hide."

"Don't put your mom and dad through this, Sara. If you run away, even more attention will be on you, and you'll be made fun of for being afraid."

"I thought you would be supportive. You're just like my mother!"

"I'm being honest with you. Gut it out, Sara. In 24 hours, this will be old news. Let's go to the mall," Sandy suggested.

"Okay."

Sara shouted. "I'm going to the mall with Sandy," as she headed to the outside door, assuming her mother had heard her. She began the three-block trip to Sandy's house. A convertible pulled up as she reached the sidewalk.

"Excuse me, excuse me! Can you help me?" asked the driver.

Sara knew enough not to talk to strangers, but the woman seemed confused and needed help. "Where is the mall around here?" the woman asked as Sara approached the vehicle.

"Let's see, you need to go..." At that moment Sara saw a GPS on the dashboard and knew the driver could easily follow the device. Uncomfortable, she stepped back a couple of paces and said, "I'm not sure."

"Certainly you must know where the mall is. Don't you and your friends hang out there?" the driver asked.

Sara said, "I'm sorry," turned and walked away in the direction opposite the vehicle. After a few seconds, the car moved on.

❀

Lou decided to go back to Traverse City, so he threw some clothes and toiletries into an overnight bag and explained to Carol that he might be gone a couple of days. He was surprised to hear that Carol wanted to go along. She had never expressed interest in going on his investigations, but this was, after all, Cherry Festival week. There would be many things to do, and shopping had to be at a premium. Carol packed a bag, and soon they were heading north. Neighbors had agreed to care for Samm and pick up newspapers and mail.

As Lou and Carol approached the city limits of Traverse City, Lou called the Laskeys to make sure Sara and at least one of her parents would be home. Lou dropped Carol off in the middle of the downtown area. Cell phones would keep them connected. Lou then drove to the Laskey home.

Sara was actually looking forward to meeting Lou. She had read several of his books, detailing past crime-solving escapades. She liked him, already trusted him, and actually wanted to help him.

Lou knocked on the door and Mrs. Laskey answered. She invited him in and Sara appeared. "Hi, Mr. Searing."

"Good morning, Sara. Thanks for meeting with me."

"I like your books."

"Oh, thank you. I enjoy writing them."

"Do you really have a dog named Samm?"

"Oh yes. Samm is a true member of the family," Lou replied with a smile. "We love her dearly."

"And, do you really walk with Mrs. Searing on the beach every evening in the summer?"

"Absolutely. We love our time together."

"I think that is so cool. And, I assume you solve all the crimes you write about?"

"What you read in my books is pretty much how it happens. I might embellish a thing or two, but the crime and how we solve it are all there."

"Cool. I'd like to meet Mr. Kelly someday."

"He'll be up here in the next few days, and I'll bring him by."

"Would you autograph your books? I have them upstairs…"

"Honey, Mr. Searing came to talk with you," Mrs. Laskey interrupted. "I am sure he hasn't the time for this."

"On the contrary, Mrs. Laskey," Lou said. "Go and get your books, Sara. I'd be happy to sign them for you."

Once he had signed the books, Lou got down to business. "Sara, I know you've talked to the police detective. You may have already answered some of my questions, but I need to hear your answers. Okay?"

"Not a problem. Will I be in your next book?" Sara asked.

"Yes, you will. That's assuming I can solve this crime."

"Oh, you will. I know you will!"

"I'm hoping you can help."

"I'll do my best." Mrs. Laskey couldn't believe the one hundred percent turn-around in Sara's attitude. Now she seemed to almost be enjoying her place in the mess which made her the center of attention.

"Let's start at the beginning. Tell me what you saw, heard, smelled, felt, tasted."

"Tasted?"

"You never know when a clue will surface. Sometimes information comes in strange forms. What I mean is, try to visualize and share the experience you had the morning of the parade."

"I was riding my bike between floats, bands, people setting up for the parade. I was near the front of the parade when I saw people scattering and screaming. I didn't see anyone shoot a gun or see the man fall over. All I saw was people in a panic. So, I decided to head toward home. I saw a woman sort of jogging toward the library. Parked in the library lot was a big motor home. When she got close to the motor home she reached in her tote bag to get keys and an object fell out. After she went in, I went over and picked up a cork. I figured she might want it, so I knocked on the door of the motor home, but there was no answer. I knew she was in there, since I saw her go in. All the windows were covered. I waited a minute and knocked again, thinking maybe she was in the bathroom or something. Again, no answer, so I rode home. I went back with my camera and took some pictures of the license plate, the mobile home."

"Why did you take photos?" Lou asked.

"I don't know. I just thought it all strange. Why didn't she answer the door? Why were all the windows covered? Why a cork in a tote bag? If this woman was there when everyone scattered and screamed, I thought a few pictures might help the police if the motor home was connected to the confusion."

"Excellent work, Sara. Do you know whether the woman saw you?"

"I don't think so, unless the window coverings were the kind that you can see out but people can't see in."

"The woman probably noticed you, especially if she was involved with the murder," Lou explained. "She may have taken a picture of you."

"I hope not."

"You were very brave. But, sometimes in being brave you put yourself in harm's way."

Mrs. Laskey, who was listening to the interview, asked, "Do you mean Sara could be in danger?"

"She could, although I doubt anything will happen. You just need to be vigilant. She shouldn't go anywhere alone. She should be with an adult at all times, at least for a while."

"Okay."

"What did you do with the cork that you found?" Lou asked.

"I brought it home and put it on my dresser. The police have it now."

"Yes, I know. And you're pretty sure the cork is what fell out of the tote bag?"

"Yes."

"It couldn't just be something that was in the grass in the area or was it in the paved library lot?"

"It was in the grass, but the grass was just cut and it was the only thing I saw fall to the ground. Do you think that little cork is important?" Sara asked.

"So far, it's the only evidence we have," Lou replied. "We can't even be sure this woman killed Mr. McNutt. She could have simply been a bystander who went quickly to her motor home and just didn't want to interact with anyone. She could be innocent. But, we know a motor home was stolen earlier that morning, and it was found in a county park a couple of hours after the shooting. So, putting two and two together, we think she is involved."

"I think she is, too."

"Sara, are you sure you saw a woman?"

"Yeah, she had a pony tail."

"Today, a pony tail doesn't always mean a woman. You didn't see her face, did you?"

"No. She was ahead of me all the time."

"But, you *are* certain the person was a woman; body-build, clothing styles…"

"I *thought* it was a woman. I never thought otherwise."

Sara suddenly turned serious. "Mr. Searing, I need to tell you something."

"What is that?" Mrs. Laskey felt the adrenaline move into her stomach.

"This morning, a woman in a car stopped me out front and asked for directions to the mall. She was in a convertible. I saw a GPS on her dashboard and figured she should be able to find the mall with that, so I walked away."

"Hmmm, thanks for telling me. Did you tell the police?" Lou asked.

"No, not even Mom."

"Did the woman resemble the woman you saw going into the motor home in any way?"

"Age maybe, but that is all."

Lou was writing on his notepad when Sara put her cell phone in front of him. It held a photo of the back of a convertible. The driver had dark short hair and her left hand was behind her head, and she wore a ring on her fourth finger.

"Quick thinking, Sara!"

"I realized I had a camera with my cell phone, so I turned back and snapped this as she drove away."

"Very good! And, I'd like to see the photos you took of the motor home."

"Do you want to see them on the desk-top computer?" Sara asked.

"That would be great."

"Let's go into Duncan's office and use his computer," Mrs. Laskey suggested.

Lou had seen the photos before, but seeing the enlarged photos, he could see-or thought he could see-a corner of a shade lifted. If he were correct, the person inside could have been watching Sara take the photo or could have been taking her own photo of Sara. He didn't share this observation so as not to alarm Sara or her mother, but he made note of it on his tablet.

⁂❀⁂

Lou had received a copy of the autopsy report that had been given to the Traverse City police. The pathologist had completed the autopsy and concluded that the cause of death was a gunshot wound. It read, "The projectile, a bullet from a .38 Special entered the body at the back, severed the spinal column between the 11th and 13th vertebrae. The bullet went on through the heart and was stopped by a rib."

Detective Morrison was studying it when Lou called.

"Hi, Lou. I trust you got the autopsy report from the pathologist? An interesting report, wouldn't you agree?"

"Yes. Shot in the back. I was under the impression that he was shot from the front," Lou admitted.

"That was my assumption as well."

"What was immediately behind the Grand Marshal's convertible?" Lou asked.

"According to the lineup sheet, it was the float carrying the Cherry Festival Queen and her court."

"Could any of them have seen the murder?" Lou asked.

"It's my opinion that they could not. The front of the queen's float comes up sort of like the bow of a boat. If the queen and her court looked straight ahead, they would only see the inside of the front of their float and nothing beyond that."

"The queen's float driver would have a good view of the Grand Marshal's vehicle in front of him, wouldn't he? If he didn't, he couldn't steer clear of the vehicle."

"You're correct. We've got to identify the driver. Wait a second, the driver was Rhonda Sheldon."

"Who is she?" Lou asked.

"She was in charge of the queen's committee this year and she always drives the queen's float."

"We need to talk to her," Lou said. "Will you contact her, or shall I?"

"I'll contact her and let you know what I find out."

"OK. Speaking of drivers, has anyone interviewed the driver of the Grand Marshal convertible?"

"Yes, Eric Williams," Detective Morrison replied. "He said he was looking forward the whole time and didn't realize Tom had been shot.

"I recall you telling me that. Okay then, let me know what you hear from the queen's driver."

Lou had turned off his cell, but he had missed a call while talking to Detective Morrison. The message was from Jerry Waters, the festival director. "Lou, please call me as soon as possible. There's another possible threat to the festival."

Lou dialed and Jerry picked up before the first ring was complete. "Thanks for calling back, Lou."

"Sure. What's up?"

"I got a call from the manager of our pit-spitting contest. A confrontation is about to take place or maybe it already has."

"What kind of confrontation?" Lou asked.

"Physical violence."

"Over what?"

"The distance a pit was spit."

"No way," Lou replied, shaking his head.

"Apparently nobody doubts where the pit landed, but the argument is over where the mouth was when the pit was expelled."

"Hey, I'm trying to solve a murder," Lou grumbled, unhappy to be interrupted with bad humor. "I don't have time for practical jokes."

"I'm serious! My staffer thinks there could be a connection to yesterday's murder."

"Okay, I'll get over to the contest venue."

"The woman calmed down and was brought to the jail to allow the crowd to settle. Trust me—it was best to remove her from the festival."

"Okay, I'll go to the jail. But, I have a hard time believing there's a connection to the murder."

"You said to let you know if something unusual happened, and that's what I did."

"Okay, okay. I'm sorry to have doubted you. Is she talking to your detectives or the county sheriff?"

"Neither at the moment. The judge is trying to arrange an attorney for her."

"Where's she from?" Lou asked.

"Belding. She's Norrie Jackson, just one of the thousands to visit the festival."

"Or, so we think. She might be involved with the killer to direct our attention away from the McNutt case. I'll go see this Laurie."

"No, Norrie. Like 'neither-nor,' Norrie."

✿❀✿

Lou went to the jail, identified himself to the deputy at the front window.

"We're expecting you. I'll buzz the door."

They walked to an interrogation room. The officer informed them, "She's with an attorney now, but he'll be coming out soon. He knows you're coming, and that you want to talk to the woman."

"Thanks."

Within a couple of minutes, Anthony Dickerson, an attorney, appeared, shook Lou's hand and said, "I understand you want to ask some questions."

"Yes."

"Fine. I'd like to be in the room with you."

"No problem. What can you tell me about Norrie? A temperamental woman? High on drugs or alcohol? Any connection to yesterday's murder?"

"I think she just lost it emotionally. She felt the contest judge didn't treat her with respect and the confrontation got ugly. She made threats, and before we knew it, people were rapidly taking sides, and a competitive spitting contest turned ugly. A connection to the murder? I doubt it, but nothing was said about that."

"Let's go in and see what we can make of it."

Lou and attorney Dickerson entered the room where Norrie waited. Lou introduced himself and led off his questioning with, "You're a pretty good spitter, uh?"

"Nope, but my son is. He's been practicing more than a year for this contest."

"What was the problem?"

"He won! He clearly won, but the judge said his mouth was over the line and disqualified him."

"What do you mean, 'His mouth was over the line'?" Lou asked, not familiar with the rules of the contest.

"You sort of lean back, and as you spit the pit, you thrust your head forward. The judge said he was over the line." Norrie moved back and then forward to demonstrate.

"You mean an *imaginary* line?"

"Yes."

"So, this is just a contest at a festival," Lou said. "No slow-motion cameras or instant-replay capability or stop-action photography?"

"No, a volunteer watches to see that all the contestants start from a common line."

The attorney added. "This isn't just a fun contest at a festival, either—this is serious. The winner goes on Letterman or Leno and demonstrates the award-winning technique. The winner has status now and at next year's festival. There are prizes and—well, no, this isn't just a fun festival contest. This is a very serious pit-spitting event."

"Okay, so you're sure your son's mouth was not over this imaginary starting line, and you disagreed with the judge."

"It wasn't just me—others near me said I was right. But, the judge gave first place to some local celebrity."

"So, an argument starts, and suddenly we have a riot on our hands?" Lou asked.

"I wouldn't say 'riot.' Sure, I was mad, but my son has been taught what is fair, and he believes if you play by the rules, you'll win. He won, and now he's told he came in second."

"Is he upset?"

"I don't think so."

"Did *he* think he went over the imaginary line?" Lou asked.

"He didn't know, but he was okay with the call. I was embarrassed for him. He asked me to leave, and we were about to, but then they arrested me. For what? I was just sticking up for my son."

"I'm investigating yesterday's murder of the Grand Marshal. I just needed to make sure there was no connection between your altercation and the murder of Mr. McNutt."

"No. I had nothing to do with that! I have a theory of why it happened, but I had nothing to do with it. It's just my theory, mind you. Everyone has a theory."

"Probably, but go ahead and tell me yours."

"In yesterday's *Record-Eagle* there was a story about a restaurant that Mr. McNutt wanted to open. But he was informed he would not be issued a drinking permit. I guess the city is at their limit. Or, other winery owners saw it as McNutt's way of bringing his wines into town and taking away a lot of their business. So, my theory is, it was revenge. McNutt probably threatened someone with harm if he didn't get his permit, and in order to avoid the threat, someone killed him."

"I see. I appreciate you talking with me. I hope you get out of this mess."

"Pardon the pun, but this is the *pits!* I was just sticking up for my son. He's a good kid. He's been working hard on his pit-spitting, and he deserved to win. He did win, fair and square."

Lou excused himself and went outside to call Jerry. He explained the results of his interview with the woman—that a simple misunderstanding got out of line.

"Thanks for the word, Lou," Jerry replied. "That's what I understood happened. We let it get out of hand, and had to get Norrie and her son out of the area to settle people down. I feel sorry for the kid. He accepted the call, and he was visibly upset with his mother carrying on like she was."

"The woman suggested the killing might relate to McNutt being denied a liquor license for a new restaurant. Have you heard this?"

"Yes, but don't waste your time. McNutt knew a couple of local eateries will be going out of business, and a license would be issued in due time. You're the investigator, but I'm sure there is no connection."

"The woman said something else that I found interesting. Perhaps the other winery owners were upset with McNutt opening a restaurant. Selling alcohol would hurt sales at their wineries. What do you think?"

"I can't comment. I'm not in the inner circle of City Council, and I know nothing about the permit process. Who provided testimony at the hearing? And who knows what the owners are saying among themselves?"

"OK. Nothing else I need?" Lou asked.

"Nothing from me."

☙❀❧

Lou went to the break room and sat down with Detective Rod Morrison. "Do you have anything I should know?" Lou asked.

"Yes, as a matter of fact, I'm leaving to interview a Mrs. Albers, who lives in a cabin on Sanford Lake. You might want to come along."

"Only if you think I can be helpful," Lou replied. "What might Mrs. Albers have to offer?"

"Her husband said she saw something on the lake. But he's skeptical, says we'll understand when we get there."

"Was it your plan to head out there?" Lou asked.

"Right after meeting with you."

"We can talk on the way."

The two drove the forty minutes to Sanford Lake and found the Albers' summer cabin.

Detective Morrison's rap on the door was answered by an elderly man. "You the police?" he asked.

"Yes, sir. I'm Detective Morrison of the Traverse City police, and this is Lou Searing, a private detective who is working with us." Lou smiled weakly and nodded.

"I'm Herm Albers," the man said as he shook their hands. "Before we go in, you need to know that Ethel is not well. When she talks, I never know whether she is making things up or living in reality. So, I caution you that she may say things that are outrageous or just something that she wants to babble about. Or, she might be right on. It depends on her medications and whether she's having a good day."

"Thanks for the heads-up," Detective Morrison said.

"Ethel is doing pretty well today. But yesterday we had the Loch Ness Monster out there," Herm said, pointing to the small, beautiful inland lake outside his back door. "I'm going to take you into the room where she lives. She never leaves our cabin. Sometimes she tells me about her life in a lighthouse, where she supposedly lives. She sits at her large window looking out on Sanford Lake and watches the 'freighters,' as she calls them. She keeps a log book and records the date, time, and weather conditions for each sighting."

"This sounds like quite a challenge for you, Mr. Albers."

"Yes, it is on occasion. She still recognizes me, has good days, and seems fairly normal most of the time. Caring for Ethel is my ministry. Jesus says in the Bible that what you do for another is the same as doing for Him. I often think of Ethel as being Jesus, and then the care-giving seems like a gift."

"You are a very loving soul," Lou said, knowing how difficult giving around-the-clock care can be.

"Let's go to her room. I really can't predict what she'll say, but she did ask me to ask the police to come out, so I did. I hope this isn't a wasted trip."

The three walked into Ethel's room, where she was seated in a straight-backed chair. The room was neat, clean, and homey. On an end table to her right was a pair of powerful binoculars, a glass of water, and a log book. Ethel was dressed in a plain dress and wearing a sweater. Her hair appeared to be recently washed.

"Ethel. The police are here. You wanted to tell them about something you saw out on the lake."

Ethel got out of her chair and turned to greet the two men. As she turned it became obvious to them that she was blind. As she put out her hand for a greeting, she glanced at the ceiling, as if wanting the sounds she heard to orient her in the room.

"Thank you for coming out. I don't remember asking Herm to call you, but I *am* glad you're here."

"We're happy to meet you," Detective Morrison said, shaking her hand. "Detective Lou Searing is with me."

Lou touched her hand so she would know to clasp it. "Nice to meet you."

"Herm, why did I ask you to call the police?"

"You said you saw something on the lake."

"Herm, would you get my log book? Do you have it?"

"Yes." Herm picked up the book.

"Please turn to July 6. About half-way down should be an entry about a rowboat."

"I found it," Herm said.

"Please read it to the police."

"I see a boat on the lake. Sailor has rowed to the middle of the lake. Drops large bag into the lake. Odd, there is no fishing pole. Wonder what's in the bag?'" Herm sounded doubtful.

"I thought the police should know about this sailor. It seems like a good way to destroy evidence, be it a body, or evidence from the scene of a crime. That's it. Thanks for coming," Ethel said cheerfully.

Ethel used her hands to find her chair, positioned herself, sat down, and returned to her world in the lighthouse.

"Can we ask her questions?" Detective Morrison asked Herm.

"You can, but as far as she's concerned, we are no longer in the room. Sorry, but that's Ethel. We've been tuned out."

"This sounds like a ridiculous question, but is she totally blind?" Lou asked.

"Yes."

"Then how could she see this boat? How can she write in her log? I don't get it."

"Neither do I. At one point, I wondered if she was mentally ill and that she saw perfectly. Maybe because of some brain malfunction, she feigned the blindness. A specialist visited and confirmed that she *is* blind."

"So, these entries in her log are her imagination?" asked Detective Morrison.

Herm pointed toward the water. "See the speedboat coming from the left. Let's see what she does with that."

They stood silent watching the boat as it slowly drifted to a stop in view of the Albers' cabin, about 200 feet from shore. A teen-aged boy dove into the water. He appeared to be diving for something without success. After a couple of minutes, he climbed back into the boat, which sped away. Ethel reached for her log. She wrote, *Speedboat on the lake. Boy dives off, perhaps to retrieve something. Finds nothing, gets back in boat with help. The boat speeds away.*

The three men stared in amazement. They left the room quietly and continued to converse in the living room. "How is that possible?" Lou asked.

"I don't know," Herm offered. "I guess it could be one of those diseases where a disability is feigned and the person truly believes he or she has a condition, but she doesn't."

"I guess the entry about the fisherman dropping a bag overboard must be true. I mean, we saw this with our own eyes. She wrote down what we saw."

"That's right, Lou," Detective Morrison replied.

"Herm, let me ask this: if we took a boat out on the lake, could she tell us the exact spot on the lake where the bag was dropped into the water?"

"I truly don't know."

"Well, we have to try. We'll come back either later today or tomorrow to see if she can help."

"Fine. She never leaves her room, so she'll be here, and so will I."

"Thank you, Herm. We'll be in touch," Detective Morrison said as the three men shook hands.

As the patrol car drove from the Albers' cabin, Detective Morrison said, "Let's go talk to the driver of the queen's float."

"Thanks for inviting me along," Lou replied, still trying to make sense out of what he had seen at the Albers' cabin.

⋇❋⋇

On their way back to Traverse City, Lou called Jack on his cell. "I need your help, Jack."

"That's what I'm here for."

"Please find information about hysterical blindness— or maybe a better term is conversion disorder. Here's the background: We've talked to a woman who appears to be blind, yet she seems to see perfectly, and can even write down what she sees. Apparently a specialist has confirmed that she is totally blind, and she behaves as if blind when you talk to her. So, we have a huge discrepancy here—a woman doing something impossible."

"I have a friend who works at Community Mental Health in Muskegon," Jack replied. "She might be able to help us."

"Thanks, Jack."

Detective Morrison contacted Chief Bixler to arrange for a boat on Sanford Lake sometime tomorrow. Unfortunately, the request couldn't have come at a worse time. The weather was perfect for water sports, and with so many tourists in town, most of the resources in the marine safety program were assigned to East Bay. Chief Bixler said, "If it doesn't need to be a craft from our fleet, I'll ask one of our volunteers to help out. Even though it's a holiday and festival week, I'm sure we'll find a boat."

✵❀✵

Christy was in her office at the Northernmost Vineyard when the phone call she dreaded came. She took a deep breath, felt her heart race, and picked up the phone. "Hello."

"Christy Johnson. You finally decided to answer the phone. Guess this is my lucky day," a deep male voice said cheerfully.

"It isn't mine, that's for sure," she responded hesitantly.

"Payback time, Christy."

"I need more time."

"We've been over this before. Time's up! I'm not getting any younger. I need my money, and I need it now."

"I know. You'll get it, but I need more time!"

"Two days. Forty-eight hours from this minute. If I don't see it in forty-eight hours, you don't want to know what I have in store for you." The phone went dead.

Christy's heart was beating rapidly. If she had ever needed Tom McNutt and his money, it was now. The winery's bank accounts were frozen and access to any funds was only by approval of the estate's attorney.

Christy called Mrs. McNutt. "Hello, Christy. How are you, dear?" Martha answered.

"I am sorry to bother you so soon after Tom's death. I know you must be terribly busy with family arriving and planning Tom's funeral, but I need help, and you are the only one who can help me."

"I'll help if I can—you know that. You're like a daughter to Tom and me. What do you need?"

"I'm in a lot of trouble, and if I don't pay a debt in forty-eight hours, I could be killed," Christy blurted out.

"Oh, my! Well, do you need a thousand dollars or something like that?" Mrs. McNutt asked.

"I need a half-million."

"A half-million? Did I hear correctly?" The amount astonished her.

"Yes, you did. *Please,* Mrs. McNutt. I'll pay you back. I really will!"

"Oh, honey, I don't *have* that kind of money."

"Maybe I shouldn't have seen your income tax report, but Tom gave it to me to file, so I know you *do* have that kind of money."

"Christy. I know you're upset, but I do *not* have money to loan you. Tom's assets are frozen. We co-own stocks, so I can't cash them in. Even if I could, paying capital gains taxes would be a huge burden at this time."

"Have you any idea where I can get the money I need?" Christy asked, deflated.

"No, I don't. I'm sorry. I'd really like to help, but I can't give you even part of that amount."

"Thanks for talking with me, Mrs. McNutt." Christy hung up, knowing the only person with the money she needed could be of no help.

CHAPTER FIVE

Detective Morrison and Lou pulled into the parking lot of the automobile dealership owned by Rhonda Sheldon, the driver of the queen's float. They walked in the front door and strolled up to the receptionist and asked for Mrs. Sheldon. The receptionist paged Rhonda who soon approached the detectives with a broad smile.

"Have you icons solved anything yet?"

"We're not icons, and no, we haven't solved anything yet," Detective Morrison said. "This is private detective, Lou Searing. He's helping us with the investigation."

"I'm pleased to meet you, Mr. Searing."

"Thank you. You've done something that's still on my bucket list."

"Sell cars?" Rhonda said, with a chuckle.

"No, drive a float in a parade."

"Oh, that. Listen, it isn't all it's cracked up to be. And, if you manage to drive behind a team of horses, it surely isn't something you want to do."

Lou and detective Morrison laughed. "I guess you have a point there," Lou remarked.

"You wanted to talk with me?" Rhonda asked, not wanting to waste any time.

Detective Morrison led with, "Yes. Your float was behind the Grand Marshal vehicle in the parade set-up area. This makes you a possible witness to the murder. Did you see anything that could help us?"

"I did see a woman with a pony tail in front of me. I look through a six-inch opening in the decorated float. I only need to make sure I'm a safe distance from the vehicle or float in front of me. I can only go straight, so I only have to see in front of me," Rhonda explained.

"I see," Detective Morrison replied.

"We were in the set-up area for quite some time before the parade started. Jerry likes us there early. Once the float is positioned, we don't need to stay with it. Usually I put on the parking brake and wander around talking to people. For me, that's the highlight of the parade. Once we start, I'm confined to the cab of the pickup and can only see straight ahead. I was behind the Grand Marshal's vehicle and not a fire truck, or as I said, the county sheriff's horseback-riding deputies."

"You said you saw a woman with a pony tail," Lou replied. "Are you sure it was a woman?"

"Are you kidding me? You think I don't know a woman when I see one?"

"It isn't that. In this day and age, a man might also have a pony tail."

"This wasn't a *man's* pony tail, Mr. Searing."

"What about a hat with hair built into it."

"What are you talking about?" Rhonda asked.

"It's a gag item. People buy them to give themselves a different look. They're popular with bald men who never got the chance for a full head of hair, or it was so long ago they've forgotten the feeling."

Rhonda looked at Detective Morrison. "Where do you *find* these characters? Is he wired like the rest of us?"

"Yes, as a matter of fact he is. I've seen one or two of these wigs."

"Must be a downstate thing. We northerners are too smart to walk around pretending to be someone we're not."

"Well, in a murder, pretending to be someone he's not is exactly what a smart criminal does."

"I see your point," Rhonda admitted. "Now that I think about it, maybe it was a fake pony tail. But nobody told me to study everyone I saw, because one of them will commit murder, and I'd need to describe everyone I saw that morning."

"Was this person with a pony tail wearing women's clothes?" Detective Morrison asked.

"Well, again, I guess anything goes these days. Let's see. I remember long pants, which I thought were a bit odd on a hot summer day. And the shirt was long-sleeved, which would hide any body hair."

"Shoes—did you happen to see her shoes?" Lou asked.

"No."

Lou continued, "Now, did this person do anything suspicious prior to the murder? Before you answer that, did you see the murder?"

"No, I did not. I think I was getting into my pickup. I had just inspected the float—air in the tires, tires free from any float material, no children under the float or in front of the tires— that sort of thing. When I got behind the wheel, I looked out my little window and saw the crowd milling around. I got out of the pickup and joined others standing near Tom as he lay in the street beside the marshal's vehicle."

"Did you hear anyone say they saw the murderer or a weapon or anything else?" Detective Morrison asked.

"No, I didn't. We were all just stunned. Then we heard sirens, and soon the paramedics were administering CPR. Some in the crowd thought he had fainted, or maybe he'd had a heart attack." There was silence while the men noted Rhonda's comment.

"Anything else I can help you with?" Rhonda asked.

"Does that six-inch window have glass or is it open?" Lou asked.

"Open. I invite mosquitoes, but I get a little air, and I get some direction from sounds. Plus, the police and parade officials can talk to me if they need to."

Lou asked, "Could the killer have shot Tom McNutt from inside your cab?"

"Yes, that's possible, and you could consider that possibility, if I weren't the driver," Rhonda stated firmly.

"Your vehicle provides something like a duck blind," Lou reasoned. "There would be no witnesses. Actually, it's a very clever arrangement—most creative."

Detective Morrison and Rhonda stood silent for a few seconds, pondering the scenario that Lou had suggested.

Rhonda, concerned, asked, "You surely don't think I killed Tom! You can't think that, because it's totally out of the question! I would feel insulted if anyone thought I would do such a thing."

"No, I *don't* think you killed Tom," Lou quickly replied. "But, someone could have gotten into your cab and shot him from there. Possible?"

"Possible, but not likely," Rhonda replied. "The pickup is totally enclosed by decorations. In fact I have to enter through a small opening near the front of the float and then inch my way up back to the cab. My mechanics take off the truck door and the windshield."

"But you said that after you are positioned, you spend most of the time out with the people," Detective Morrison reminded Rhonda.

"That's right."

"So, someone who knows the set-up could get in the cab, fire the shot, and leave during the commotion," Lou replied.

"I guess that's possible," Rhonda admitted. "But, I don't think it happened."

"But, my point is, it *could* have. Correct?" Lou asked.

"Yes, I guess it could have," Rhonda agreed, shaking her head in disbelief.

⁂

One thing on Lou's mind was the comment by Martha Mc-Nutt that Fr. Pat wouldn't be able to say anything about Tom's annulment. To Lou, the word "annulment" signaled potential conflict. It may not mean conflict, but it is a significant event in the lives of Catholics who wish to annul a marriage. According to Martha, Tom was involved with the annulment process, yet he was not Catholic. That meant that his former spouse could be Catholic and wanted an annulment before Tom was murdered.

While Lou was working with Detective Morrison, Carol was doing some serious shopping. Special sales made her hunt all the more interesting and enticing. If every visitor spent half as much as Carol, the famous vacation land of Michigan would have more dollars coming in than grains of sand on the beach.

The day was coming to an end, and while the case seemed a long way from being solved, as long as information was flowing and people cooperated, Lou could call it a good day.

❧❀❧

The killer was monitoring the news coming out of Traverse City on both television and the Internet. She was pleased that nothing of significance was being reported, but the thirteen year-old girl who had seen a suspect and picked up the cork gave her heartburn. The kid was the only thing standing between a perfect crime and life in prison. The words 'seen the suspect' were most disturbing, and the police having the cork was also troublesome.

The killer knew that staying in one spot longer than a day or two meant leaving a trail. So it was time to move on. She would leave in the morning. All the evidence was at the bottom of the lake, and as far as she knew, the law had no idea *where* she was, or *who* she was, unless the young witness may have seen enough to pick her out of a lineup.

❧❀❧

Lou and Carol planned to eat dinner at Bower's Harbor Inn on the Old Mission Peninsula. They had often dined at that unique restaurant when they came to the Traverse City area for an annual Special Education Administrators' Conference.

After dinner, they planned to visit Interlochen Music Camp southwest of Traverse City. The talent of the young campers and the year-round academic students is nothing short of amazing. On this evening, Lou and Carol would hear the World Youth Symphony. If ever a concert would make one feel good about our youth, this was it. For Lou, good food, the sun setting on Green Lake, an evening with Carol, and marvelous music was another definition of Heaven.

CHAPTER SIX

Day 3 • July 8

As luck would have it, a room was available when Carol called Wellington Inn Bed and Breakfast in downtown Traverse City. The elegant inn was perfect for a getaway. Information on the Internet introduced the reader to a unique setting. The inn was a wonderful place to relax.

The breakfast was elegant. Lou was a cheerios-toast-cranberry juice type of guy, so the delicious food was not only tasty but varied and each guest had something different, from crepes to French toast. Carol enjoyed every minute of the meal. After breakfast, she decided to catch a few more winks, while Lou left to pursue the killer of the town's philanthropist.

Jack and Elaine were to arrive today. Elaine and Carol had planned shopping with lunch at the Hanna Bistro. Jack was sure that Lou had his day planned, and he was eager to get to on-the-scene research.

Lou looked forward to visiting Ethel and learning what she might see on Sanford Lake when a boat mimicked the dumping incident. Later, he would take a trip up the Mission Peninsula to learn about wine-making. Finally, he would attend the wake/viewing for Tom McNutt, hoping to meet people who could either offer helpful details or give him names of people to interview later. He had a feeling that, before he kissed Carol good night, he would have an idea who the killer was.

⋇❀⋇

During the morning, Detective Morrison would be with Herm and Ethel as a rowboat with a lone man, no fishing pole, and a large heavy bag was to come into view. The effort would be for Ethel to help Detective Morrison know where the boat was located when the boater dumped the bag into the lake. Lou would be with the sheriff's department volunteer who was instructed to row the boat out into the middle of the lake and stop. Lou and Detective Morrison would be in touch via cell phone.

The morning was clear and bright. Lou called Rod Morrison to be sure that Ethel was in her chair and looking at the lake. Once that was confirmed, a sheriff's volunteer rowed out into the lake from a public access ramp. As the boat came into view, Ethel took her powerful binoculars, lifted them to her eyes, and watched for a good two or three minutes.

When the volunteer got to the middle of the lake, he pulled the oars into the boat, sat quietly for a minute, looked around, and then dropped the weighted bag over the side of his boat. He then waited another minute before rowing back to his starting point.

Ethel set the binoculars down carefully and picked up her log. Herm watched as she printed. *9:16 a.m. Rowboat, one man, no fishing pole, dropped a bag into the lake. This is the second time this has happened. Both boats were in the same general area.*

Herm asked her to describe what she had seen, and she responded that she had not seen anything. He reminded her about the entry in her log about seeing a boat with a lone rower. Ethel simply sat, staring out her window, saying nothing.

Herm and Detective Morrison exchanged glances, and each shrugged his shoulders. How can this be? Detective Morrison thought. *She has been declared legally blind, yet she sees things with binoculars and records what she sees in a log.*

Detective Morrison called Lou to explain what had happened, and he too, was astonished. "Well, at least we confirmed what she said about a boat with a single rower who dropped a bag into the water. The next step is to send divers down and hope they can see both bags or at least one of them. Maybe the bag is full of trash, or maybe it contains evidence."

"Well, one thing is for sure," Detective Morrison replied. "The bags aren't going anywhere, so we don't need to do that immediately."

"That's right. Let's head back to town to meet Jack for lunch. Please thank Herm and Ethel for me."

≈✿≈

Early in the afternoon Lou, Jack, and Detective Morrison drove north along the Old Mission Peninsula, a narrow strip of land separating Grand Traverse Bay into West and East Arms. Not only does the Peninsula provide an exquisite scenic drive, but it also is home to many first-class wineries. The three men stopped at all seven wine-tasting sites, not to taste, but to get a cork from each.

The main mission was to visit Northernmost Winery and talk again with Christy. When they arrived at that winery, they encountered a huge sign that read, *Winery temporarily closed in memory of Tom McNutt, our owner, friend, and public servant.* The driveway to the office was open, so the men drove back to the headquarters. They could see workers in the vineyards and processing buildings, but there were no visitors.

At the office door, they were greeted by a man who appeared to be in a maintenance uniform. "Sorry, gentlemen, we're closed. Did you miss the sign out by the road?"

"We saw it. We're investigating the death of Mr. McNutt," Lou began. "I'm Lou Searing and I talked to Christy the afternoon of the murder. These are Detective Morrison of the Traverse City Police and my assistant, Jack Kelly." Both men nodded as Lou mentioned their names.

"Well, Miss Christy isn't here. She took the day off. She's been pretty stressed out, as you can imagine. She wants to go to the funeral home this afternoon or evening and wanted to rest before then."

"I see. Do you mind if we talk with you?" Lou asked.

"That'd be okay I guess. I'm Stone Elliott."

"Stone?" Lou asked to make sure he had heard correctly.

"Yes. My mom thought I'd be rolling all my life so as not to grow moss. At least that's what she says when people ask her about my name."

"Pleased to meet you," Lou said, noting the name in his notebook. "We just have a few questions."

"Talking to me is probably a waste of your time. I work out in the maintenance shed, wouldn't recognize Mr. McNutt if he walked in the door. I see his name on my paycheck, but that's about all I know about him."

"Could we come in?" Detective Morrison asked.

"I guess you can. There's nothing to see. This building has some offices, lots of records, and files. Actually, all the office staff took the afternoon off. They left me in charge, which is kind of scary, but when you close the place, there's not a lot to being in charge."

"We'd like to look around. Would that be okay?" Jack asked.

"Being that you're the law, I guess that'd be okay. Nothing but offices. Sure, come on in."

Once inside, the three split up. Lou went into Mr. McNutt's office. Jack headed to the clerical area, where the business manager worked alongside a bookkeeper. Detective Morrison went into Christy's office. Because they didn't have a search warrant, they were careful not to open any drawers or cabinets or to remove anything. They simply observed the layout of the operation.

On the walls were countless awards: photos of Tom with dignitaries, and plaques expressing appreciation for years of service on this or that board. Photos of celebrities decorated Tom's large walnut desk. Lou thought it odd that there was no photo of Mrs. McNutt or Mercy. He stood behind the desk and glanced at the top phone note in a short pile. *Call Jerry Waters about Grand Marshal float.* A number followed. He noticed a message light on the phone. He wished he could listen to it, but knew he couldn't. He needed a search warrant for that, and he'd make sure Detective Morrison talked to Chief Bixler about it.

Christy's office was very neat. The only thing on her desk was a thick booklet with the words, 'Northernmost Winery Audit.' Jack jotted the name of the auditing firm. Other than the audit report there were no phone messages, and the message light was dark. Jack couldn't see anything of interest in the business manager's office.

The three thanked Stone for allowing them in. Lou said, "I'll see Christy tonight at the viewing, and I'll tell her we stopped and that you were helpful."

"Thank you."

"One more thing before we leave. Could you answer a question?"

"If I can."

"I saw a lot of photos around Mr. McNutt's desk, but I didn't see any of Mrs. McNutt. In fact, here is one with Tom and Christy at a golf outing."

"I haven't a clue," Stone replied.

Lou thought of Martha McNutt at St. Joe's. *Maybe she is seeking an annulment; maybe Tom wouldn't go along with it, so she killed him.*

"Thanks for your help, Stone. We'll be on our way."

"Goodbye now."

"One more thing, could we have a cork from your winery?"

"I guess so. Why do you need it?"

"I collect them."

"You and a thousand other people. I'll get one. Please wait here."

"Thank you."

※❀※

With cork in hand, the three detectives stopped at a restaurant for a late lunch. After placing their order, Jack said, "I researched conversion disorder. Is this a good time to explain what I found?"

"As good as any," Lou replied. "Go ahead."

"Since Ethel is blind, but doesn't appear to be so, let me use her as an example. First of all, conversion disorder occurs more often in women than in men, and it almost always follows a traumatic event in the life of the patient. In your case, Ethel might have witnessed something horrific. A 'blind' person with conversion disorder is not really blind, but she *thinks* and *acts* as if she is. She may even exhibit mannerisms of someone who is blind."

"So, she *thinks* she's blind, but isn't really," Lou mused. "Does she just see what she wants to see?"

"Usually a CD person can see everything you and I see. They store impressions in the brain, and have a memory of seeing it. But outwardly, the patient *thinks* she is blind and therefore *acts* as if she's blind."

"So, if she has this conversion disorder, she *did* see the person in the boat drop a bag into the water, could write legibly in her log, but can't talk about it, because in her mind, she didn't see anything."

"Correct," Jack replied nodding his head. "That's how I would interpret these circumstances."

Detective Morrison asked, "Do people grow out of this?"

"As I understand it, they do get better, and can eventually recover. But recovery is related to the severity of the disease, the effectiveness of treatment, and the general health of the patient."

Lou summarized, "I think she records in her log what she really sees, and what she writes really happened, based on this morning's experiment. I'm convinced that a lone man in a rowboat did drop a bag in the middle of the lake. Now, whether this is related to our case is another question. Chances are, it's not, but stranger things have happened."

⁂

The killer decided she shouldn't kidnap the girl who had seen her. She reasoned that she was lucky enough to have committed the perfect crime, and to expect another successful murder was pressing her luck. She also decided to keep moving, for the more frequently she did, the less likely the authorities would be on her trail. She straightened the cabin, raked the outside area, pulled the boat up on shore, and put her belongings in her car. She left a nightlight on to give the impression the place was occupied and then drove away.

Detective Morrison called Chief Bixler and requested a search warrant for the office and home of Tom McNutt. The process had already begun and the chief was awaiting word from the judge.

Once back in town, Detective Morrison bade Lou good-bye and thanked him for a profitable day of investigation. Lou and Jack had a half-hour before they were to meet Carol and Elaine. The name of the winery's tasting room, Left Foot Charley, caught their attention and they went in.

They sat at the wine-tasting bar and began to talk with Marti, the sales representative who was pouring small portions for visitors to taste.

"I'm not a wine aficionado," Lou said, feeling like a fish out of water. "What do you recommend for a man with a sweet tooth who doesn't enjoy alcohol?"

Marti laughed, "You would probably be best to find a Hershey candy bar. Much of our wine will curl your tongue." Jack laughed at Lou's bumbling around.

"Would you please bring me a bottle of your cherry wine?" Lou asked. "I'd like to see the label." Marti brought Lou a bottle, and he carefully read the label. "If you don't mind, I have a few questions. You go ahead and serve your customers, and when you have a free moment, come to us and help us understand this industry. Would you do that?"

"Sure. I hope I can answer your questions. It is kind of slow right now, so ask me something."

"Let's start at the top, literally. Where does a winery like yours get the corks that go in the bottles?"

"Corky. He's the sales rep for a large company in Portugal. He travels all around the country selling corks. I assume Corky is a nickname. His name is Cornelius, so I think it was a childhood nickname that stuck. He just happened to become a cork salesman."

"How often does he come by?"

"Not often. Most of the sales are made electronically and we don't need to see Corky. Now that I think about it, he hasn't been by in quite some time."

"Do other wineries in the area buy their corks from him?" Jack asked.

"He has a corner on the area market. First of all, the cork is of high quality. Also, they stamp our insignia on each cork, and we like that. Finally, the price is right. So Corky gets our business."

Lou nodded. "Okay. Tell me about the bottles."

"They're ordered from a distributor in Virginia. In our case we order them by the thousands."

"How about other wineries? Do they order from the same distributor?"

"I don't know for sure, but I am inclined to think we order from various companies. Each of our bottles has a distinct design."

"Is there another salesperson like Corky who comes by to sell?"

"No, Corky is about the only traveling sales representative, and he goes back a long time. Nowadays salespeople call the wineries, suggest we order from their website, and have our orders shipped. Unless we have a problem, we don't see a human being."

Marti left to pour wine for a tour group coming into the tasting room. Lou thought he'd not be able to talk with Marti again, but she was efficient and came back to Lou and Jack shortly.

"All right, labels. Where do they come from?" Lou asked.

"Right here in Traverse City. We work with a graphic design artist to give us a unique visual. There are so many wines available these days, we need to attract customers with something unique. The label has adhesive on the back, and we hire a person part-time to apply the labels."

"Lastly, the wine. Are all the grapes grown in your vineyards?" Lou asked.

Marti paused as if she was thinking of how to answer a delicate question. "Most wineries use their own grapes, but sometimes they buy grapes or other fruits from suppliers. Some of the grapes come from southwest Michigan, the Paw Paw area. Some wineries bring in grapes from as far away as California."

"Is this legal?" Jack asked.

"The key is the label," Marti replied. "If the label says Michigan grapes, we are okay. But if we *imply* Michigan grapes when they *really* come from somewhere *else,* that's not ethical."

"I see," Lou replied. "Thank you very much for answering our questions, Marti. I'd like to buy a bottle of your cherry wine to give to friends who enjoy wine with their meals. Just choose one, and I'll pay for it with my credit card."

Lou and Jack walked out of Left Foot Charley's with a bottle of Traverse City wine and considerably more understanding of the wine industry.

In late afternoon, Jack, Elaine, Lou, and Carol went out for a light meal in downtown Traverse City. Lou planned to go to the funeral home immediately after eating, and Jack would go along in case Lou wanted something done. Carol and Elaine decided to remain downtown for some of the Cherry Festival music events.

⟡❀⟡

The killer planned to head toward the Mackinac Bridge after a stop at the funeral home in Traverse City to pay respects. She didn't expect any trouble because, as far as she knew, she was not a suspect. Police would not be looking for her model of car or her license plate. The longer she was free, the more confidence she gained, and the feeling of freedom was exhilarating.

⟡❀⟡

There was a huge crowd at the McNutt viewing. The lines to sign the guest book, or to make memorial donations to a long list of charities that Martha McNutt had identified, snaked throughout the entrance to the room where Tom's closed casket sat on a bier.

Lou and Jack didn't stand in line, but walked directly into the funeral home where Tom lay. There were flowers everywhere, adding to a festive air of hundreds of people sharing hugs, memories, and condolences.

Lou quickly spotted Mrs. McNutt and joined the line to pay his respects. Earlier he had asked Jack to keep an eye on Christy, noting who she talked with and her demeanor. Jack was also to note who had sent flowers, especially the largest displays.

As Lou's line inched ahead, he glanced to his right and saw Sara Laskey with her mother and father. Sara looked at Lou and each nodded. Lou finally reached Mrs. McNutt. In an effort to try and discover exactly who she was, Lou said, "I'm Lou Searing, assisting the police in solving Tom's death. I remember talking with you, but I can't recall where; I've talked to many people in many different places in the last few days. Please accept my sincere sympathy at your loss."

"Thank you, Mr. Searing. We met at the hospital fairly soon after Tom was pronounced dead.

"Yes, of course. And, you told me your daughter had said Tom didn't have an enemy in the world."

"Yes, I did say that. Actually, his daughter is from Tom's first marriage."

"I see. And then I saw you at St. Joe's when I stopped to see Father Pat."

"Yes. Mr. Searing, there are hundreds here to talk with me. Thank you for coming and for your kind words. Perhaps we can talk another time, under less stressful circumstances."

"I understand. Again, I'm sorry for your loss."

"Thank you." Lou shook her hand warmly and moved to greet Sara and her parents.

"Good evening, Sara," Lou said. "I didn't expect to see you here."

"To be honest, I didn't want to come," Sara whispered. "These places are creepy. My parents thought I was old enough

to experience a wake. Talk to the police, go see a dead man…"
Sara's voice rose. "Mr. Searing, I can't take much more of this.
Can't I just be a teenager?"

"Let me tell you a secret I learned years ago. My sister taught
it to me and it has come in very handy. When you don't want to
be somewhere, send an invisible friend to handle the situation.
Then you just relax and ride it out."

"That sounds spooky. I don't get it."

"OK, follow me. You're here in this funeral home. Just accept
it—it's where you are. But, in your imagination, you aren't here,
because you sent someone to represent you. Now you're free to
play detective, for example. That's what Jack and I are doing."

"Really?"

"Oh yes, we're constantly looking for clues."

"What kind of clues?"

"Who isn't here that should be? Who is here, but acting a
bit strangely? We'll walk out and look at the guest register, to
see who came and who may have come together. There's a lot
to see and hear."

"Cool. I'm going to try it," Sara said, brightening up. "Now,
I guess I should show some manners. Dad, this is Mr. Searing.
Mr. Searing this is my father, Duncan Laskey."

"I'm pleased to meet you, Mr. Searing."

"Please call me, Lou. Your daughter is delightful."

"Thank you. I've heard a lot of adjectives describing Sara, but 'delightful' has seldom been one of them," Duncan said while giving his daughter playful hug.

"Well, thanks, Dad!"

"Well, she is," Lou replied as Sara gave him a thumbs up. "In fact, my money is on her playing a big part in solving this case."

"That would be a feather in her cap."

"And you folks are here this evening because…?" Lou asked.

"I did business with Tom McNutt, and we were in Rotary together," Duncan replied.

"What kind of business?"

"I sell cleaning supplies, and Tom was always a good customer."

"I see. Well, I've got other people to talk to, so please excuse me," Lou said before seeing Sara's mother looking at a picture board. "Oh, Mrs. Laskey. I didn't mean to ignore you. Good evening." Mrs. Laskey smiled, nodded, and went back to looking at the photos of Tom on display.

Just before Lou left, he got Sara's attention and said quietly, "Take this lemon and make lemonade." Sara smiled.

Jack could not find Christy. He checked the registration book, but did not see her name. But he encountered Stone Elliott, the maintenance man he'd met earlier in the day at the winery. Jack approached him. "We meet again."

"Yes. I figured I should come this evening. Mr. McNutt did a lot to help me. He didn't lay me off—I would be homeless if he hadn't kept me on."

"Did he lay off anyone else?" Jack asked.

"Oh, yes. A few months ago, he fired our brew master and two production employees."

"How did they take that disruption in their lives?"

"Not well. Not that anybody takes that sort of news well. Christy had to do the dirty work and tell them they were no longer working for the winery. Let's just say it was quite tense around the vineyard."

"I can imagine," Jack replied. "What were their names?"

"The brew master was Heather Adams. The two production workers were Dennis Smith and Anthony Kellogg." Jack noted their names on a file card.

"Do they live in the Traverse City area?"

"I'm not sure. I think they live on a lake outside Traverse City, but I could be wrong."

"Well, you didn't come here to talk with me. Nice of you to pay your respects to Mrs. McNutt."

"It's something I needed to do."

Jack asked a distinguished-looking older man if anyone in the funeral home was on the winery's board of directors. The gentleman pointed out a woman seated by the coffin who was president of the board. She was tearing up as she talked with people who appeared to know her. Jack passed this information to Lou, who approached and waited for a moment when she was alone.

"Excuse me. I'm Lou Searing. I'm helping the Traverse City police with the investigation of Mr. McNutt's murder. I understand you're on the board of the Northernmost Winery?"

"Yes. I'm Violet Tomlinson."

"You surely didn't come here to talk to an investigator, but I didn't want to miss the opportunity to meet you."

"I understand. But what do you think I can tell you?" Violet asked.

"I'm curious whether there was any tension on the board, specifically, any tension involving Tom?"

"Don't go there, Lou."

"That bad, huh?"

"I refer to your suggestion that someone on the Board had a role in Tom's death. Nothing could be further from the truth."

"Okay. I'm just asking. Any idea who might have killed this man?"

"We all think we know who killed him, so I do have my hunch."

"Would you mind sharing that hunch?" Lou asked.

"Christy Johnson."

"Because?"

"She had everything to gain from having him out of the way."

"For example?"

"Full control of the winery, for one. Then revenge for having had to tell three of our most valuable and loyal employees that they were fired. And, finally forcing her to become involved with potentially illegal practices."

"Illegal practices?" Lou asked.

"I don't want to comment further. Just know that everything was not on the up-and-up."

"Thanks," Lou said. "You've been helpful."

"Don't let Christy know that I pointed my finger at her. She'd kill me."

"Literally or figuratively?" Lou asked.

"That's a good question," Violet replied without a hint of a smile.

"Could I please ask you a question about Tom's family?"

"Certainly."

"Forgive me, this is very personal; but was Tom having an affair?"

"One never knows, but I would say, definitely not. I know Martha quite well, and she would tell me if she suspected it. But, as I said, one never really knows."

Lou continued. "Was Tom married before he married Martha?" Lou asked, knowing the answer, but wondering what he might learn.

"I'm pretty sure he was. I recall Tom mentioning to me that his first wife left him. Said something like, 'I woke up one morning, a note was on the pillow, and she was gone.' I knew she was Catholic, and according to Tom, she was always bugging him to join the Catholic church, but he wouldn't hear of it."

"So, they divorced, and now there is Martha."

"I didn't say there was a divorce. Tom never used that word."

"So, he was married before, was married to Martha when he was killed, and you have not heard of a mistress."

"That's what I understand."

"By any chance, do you know where Joanne lives if she is still living."

"Greenville, Michigan, and as far as I know, she is still alive.

"I won't keep you any longer. Thanks for talking with me. Here is my card if you wish to talk with me later."

Jack checked the huge displays of flowers, but the donor's names meant nothing to him. He looked at the large display of photos of Tom at various stages of his life and the awards he'd won. Again, nothing that might help with the investigation caught his eye.

Jack and Lou met in the lobby and concluded that they had gained all they could from the gathering. Carol and Elaine were to have left for home in Jack's car. Lou and Jack would leave later.

Jack was driving, approaching the Whitehall/Montague Exit when Lou's cell phone rang. Lou answered and heard a worried voice say, "Lou, this is Duncan Laskey. Sara is missing. When we were ready to leave the funeral home we couldn't find her."

"Did she have her cell phone with her?"

"I assume so, yes."

"Have the police been notified?"

"Oh, yes. They're doing all they can."

"I hope they're checking the guest list at the funeral home. And, they should be able to locate that cell phone. Who have you been dealing with in the police department?" Lou asked.

"Detective Morrison. He's sure they'll find Sara. But, our worst fear is that the McNutt killer has kidnapped and might kill her."

"I'll call Detective Morrison to make sure they're tracing the cell phone, and I'll call you when I learn anything new."

Rod Morrison responded that the police did have the guest list, and the phone had been found about ten feet from US 31 south of Elk Rapids and would be dusted for prints. The location of the phone indicated that the vehicle was headed north.

"I've put out a be-on-the-lookout bulletin for a vehicle with two occupants, one a teenage girl. I'm hoping that Sara is alive."

"Did Jack tell you he took photos of all the cars in the funeral home parking lot?"

"Yes, and I have those photos. We've put that list on the BOL bulletin."

"Jack and I are driving back to Grand Haven. I'll have my cell phone on, so please call as soon as you learn anything more."

✿❀✿

Sara regained consciousness in the trunk of a vehicle. The vehicle was not moving, but she ached all over. She had tape over her mouth. Her arms were tied together behind her and her feet were tied at the ankles. She thought, *Am I dreaming, or is this really happening?*

Sara realized that her head was on a pillow. She could see and hear and feel tape across her mouth, and rope cutting painfully into her skin when she moved. When she heard two doors slam shut, she deduced that two people were in the car. As the vehicle moved, she felt pain with every bump in the road.

Kidnapping Sara was premeditated, but not at the funeral home. The killer did not expect to see the girl at the funeral home, but the opportunity presented itself to leave town with the one person preventing the perfect crime and she couldn't pass it up.

The killer was smart enough to take Sara's phone and, like an apple core, throw it from the car on northbound US 31. She was also smart enough not to sign the guest book or to stay more than the minute or two it took to entice Sara from the funeral home. Finally, she had replaced her license plate with one stolen in the city. But she didn't realize that Jack had taken several photos of the plates of cars in the parking lot with his cell phone.

The car was heading for the Mackinac Bridge. The rope around her wrists was loose enough for Sara to try to break free. She tore skin on her wrists, but with persistence she was able to free her hands. Then she untied her ankles and removed the tape from her mouth. She had no idea where she was or what might happen to her, but it wasn't anything good, that much she knew.

In the dark, she was able to find a tire iron. She knew someone would eventually open the trunk. At that point she might be able to attack using the tire iron as a weapon, hoping the kidnappers did not have a gun.

Sara felt the car move more slowly for a minute or two before coming to a stop. The next thing she knew, the trunk lid was opened and two people, a man and a woman, tried to pull her out. She swung the tire iron back and forth, kicking and screaming, and managed to escape. As Sara ran down the road, she realized the vehicle had stopped on the Mackinac Bridge.

Apparently her kidnappers intended to dump her into the Straits of Mackinac. As she ran, she got the attention of drivers, but not one of them stopped. Thwarted, the kidnappers got back into the car and sped toward the north end of the bridge.

At Bridge headquarters, a bridge-cam clearly showed Sara frantically running south in the twilight, against the flow of northbound traffic. Within a minute, a State Police cruiser with lights flashing pulled to a stop. The trooper got out of the vehicle and Sara ran into his arms. "Help me, help me," she pleaded.

"You're okay, you're okay," he assured her. Sara continued to cling to the trooper. "Get into my car. You'll be safe there." He opened the back door of the cruiser, and Sara collapsed against the upholstery. She took a deep breath and let out a long sigh.

The Bridge Authority closed the lanes at the north exits, so no vehicles could continue north. The long lines in four lanes left drivers wondering about the closure. The authorities had no idea in which car the girl had been held captive. Apparently witnesses were reluctant to inform them about the car stopped near the center of the Bridge, or of the confrontation in the northbound lane.

Finally cars were allowed through, and video cameras were positioned to record the cars at the toll booths. The State Police pulled over suspicious vehicles, questioned the occupants and searched the trunks. Toll workers looked carefully at the occupants of each car and the interior for any clues as the toll transaction was completed. Since Sara had been in the trunk, there was nothing to observe in the kidnapper's car. This didn't matter, as the killer's vehicle wasn't identified as suspicious and was waved through.

The trooper drove Sara to the office of a physician in Mackinaw City who made herself available when the State Police needed medical assistance. While *en route* he had asked dispatch to have a female trooper meet him at the doctor's office. The base commander called the Traverse City police to report that Sara Laskey was safe in Mackinaw City, although she appeared traumatized by her ordeal.

State Police arranged for Mr. and Mrs. Laskey and Detective Morrison to fly by helicopter to Mackinaw City. The reunion at the doctor's office was quite emotional. Sara was never so glad to see her parents, and one could almost see her become herself again after the reunion. The doctor, Dr. Helen Mirras, met with everyone and offered her evaluation.

"I examined Sara and found no evidence of molestation. She has abrasions on her wrists and ankles from being tied with coarse rope. She is traumatized by her experience, but I have seen much improvement since you folks have been with her."

✿

Approaching Muskegon, Lou's cell phone rang; Detective Morrison was calling.

"Lou, I'm calling from Mackinaw City. Sara has been found safe. She was kidnapped in Traverse City, driven in a car trunk onto the Mackinac Bridge. Her abductors planned to throw her into the Straits, but she escaped. She's shaken by the ordeal, but the doctor says she'll be fine. State police have been extremely helpful. A helicopter brought Mr. and Mrs. Laskey and me up here. We're fairly sure that the car that was carrying Sara went through the north toll booth, and we hope surveillance video helps us identify the vehicle."

"Good news on all fronts!" Lou replied. "Please tell Sara and her parents that Jack and I are thankful she's okay, and that I'll see them tomorrow."

"Will do, Lou."

"Thanks for calling, Rod."

❀❀❀

Lou called the commander of the State Police Post in St. Ignace. After explaining who he was and his role in the investigation, Lou asked, "Can I get a copy of the video of cars approaching and leaving the toll booths?"

"Yes, Chief Bixler gets it first, but I imagine she will get it to you."

"We've collected lots of photos of vehicles, so I am curious to see if one of them appears in your videos. We have license plate photos I want to compare as well."

"Once you get a description, let us know through Chief Bixler if you need a car found and we'll put out a BOL for our staff, and also for Canadian authorities."

"Thanks. I would imagine *someone* saw Sara struggling to get away from her captors."

"Yes, I'm sure they did," the commander agreed.

"Has anyone contacted you?" Lou asked.

"Not yet. My guess is the witnesses don't want to get involved. They're heading for vacation spots or hunting and don't want to take the time to be interviewed."

"It's my guess someone's conscience will drive them to contact you," Lou said.

"I agree. I hope so."

"Thanks for talking with me. I'll talk to Sara tomorrow in Traverse City, and I look forward to getting the videos from Chief Bixler."

⚘

As he neared Grand Haven, Lou decided to try to talk to Sara, late as it was. He dialed Mr. Laskey, who answered, much to Lou's surprise. Lou asked if he might talk to Sara.

"She's right here and I'm sure she would love to hear from you."

"Hello." Sara sounded tired but relaxed.

"Sara, I can't tell you how thankful I am that you're okay," Lou said sincerely.

"Yes, I think I would have been thrown off the Bridge."

"You were smart and very brave. I'm proud of you!"

"Just common sense and wanting to get away," Sara replied.

"I know you've talked to your parents and Detective Morrison but, if you can handle it, I'd like you to tell me what happened."

"Okay. I was sitting in the funeral home, doing as you suggested, letting my imaginary friend take over the social stuff while I played detective. A man came up and said something like, 'Would you please help me? I have some things in my car that should go to Mrs. McNutt. I need help carrying them in.'"

"An innocent enough request," Lou replied.

"I know. So I went with him out to his car. He opened the trunk, asked me to reach in for the package. And then, before I knew it, I was in the trunk, the lid slammed shut, and the car was moving. Later we stopped in some secluded place where they tied me up, taped my mouth shut, and shoved me back in the trunk."

"*They?* Two men, two women, or a man and a woman?" Lou asked.

"A man and a woman."

"Did you recognize them?"

"No."

"Can you describe the car?" Lou asked.

"You know, I can't," Sara said, puzzled. "It was yellow, but that's about all I remember."

"Can you describe the man?"

"He was middle-aged, he wasn't fat, he was wearing long pants, and he had hair. I couldn't see his face because he had a mask on, but I don't think he had a beard."

"And the woman?"

"She was tall and thin. I didn't see her face, but she could have been the woman who went to the motor home. I don't know. Maybe not. It happened so fast that I didn't take the time to get a good look at either of them."

"Jack took photos of all the vehicles in the funeral home parking lot," Lou said. "Chances are good that the car might be in one of them. If we compare the cars in the videos taken at the Bridge toll booths with cars in the funeral home parking lot, we should be able to find a match, if there is one, in short order."

"How are you feeling now, Sara," Lou asked.

"I'm okay. It seems like I had a nightmare. My wrists and ankles hurt, but I'll be fine."

Lou then asked to speak privately with Detective Morrison. "Yes, Lou."

"I think Sara and at least one of her parents should go some place where she'll be safe, at least till we get this solved."

Morrison agreed. "We'll take care of that as soon as possible, probably in the morning."

The helicopter carrying the Laskeys and Detective Morrison to Traverse City landed in about the same time Lou pulled into his garage in Grand Haven. The illuminated digital clock in Lou's car read 12:40 a.m.

CHAPTER SEVEN
Day 4 • July 9

Very early in the morning, Detective Morrison stayed with the Laskey family while Sara and her mother collected clothes and toiletries, books, and materials to keep them occupied for a few days. They then rode in an unmarked car to Northport, at the north end of the Leelanau Peninsula, to stay in a cabin rented by the week. There they were isolated and could go into public places like any tourists to shop for groceries. This was not far from Traverse City so Mr. Laskey could visit whenever he wanted, or he could stay there if he wished.

꙰❀꙰

While Lou was not one to sleep in, he did this day, for yesterday had been a long day. When he finally arose, Carol had been up for a few hours. She left a note that she had gone to the club to exercise, and then would stop at the Farmers' Market. Lou showered, dressed and headed for the kitchen. He had no calls on his cell and no phone messages, so he opened his e-mail on the kitchen computer. There were 23 messages, but not one of them was important.

Lou had planned to work out of his home for a day or two, but that was before Sara was kidnapped. As long as the drive was, he felt he needed to be in Traverse City. The Cherry Festival was winding down, so getting a motel room wouldn't be too difficult. He packed some clothes and toiletries, left a note for Carol, and headed north.

En route he called Detective Morrison for the latest information about Sara's kidnapping.

"We've found Mrs. Laskey and Sara a small cottage in Northport, Lou."

"Okay. Is anything else going on?" Lou asked.

"We got the search warrant, so now we can make a thorough search at the Northernmost Winery. I assume you want to go along?"

"Yes, I would. I'll let you know when I get to town, probably around noon."

Lou had no more than finished his call when he heard from Carol.

"How is your trip going?"

"I'm tired, but okay I guess. How is your day going?" Lou asked.

"I heard about a great deal."

"I'm curious and scared at the same time. What is it?"

"Are you up for a move to Manistee?" Carol asked.

"No, but tell me more."

"I found a Lake Michigan lakefront home for sale. It sounds perfect for us. I took a video tour on the Internet."

"You don't like our home in Grand Haven?" Lou asked.

"Oh no, I love our home, but I think we could sell it easily. We could pay for the Manistee home and have money left over for travel or whatever we want to do."

"So, it's an economic thing," Lou replied.

"Right."

"Wouldn't you miss friends, church and your exercise club?"

"Probably, but we'd make new friends and adjust to a new church and find another exercise facility. But, Grand Haven is your hometown, so I suppose you don't want to leave?"

"I have no need to stay, either. Let's look into it. One thing I'd really miss is being near my sister when she comes up to her cottage in the summer."

"You're right," Carol said. "I think Gayle is reason enough to stay in Grand Haven."

"Does this place have an office with a view of Lake Michigan?" Lou asked.

"As a matter of fact, it does," Carol replied. "And, there's even a room for my quilting. Actually, the house has bigger rooms for our studios."

"Cool," Lou said, sounding more interested with each passing moment.

"It's just something to think about. Have a good trip, Lou."

"Okay. I'll be in touch. Love you. Bye."

༄❀༄

The Traverse Bay County Marine Search and Rescue Patrol was not as busy now that the Cherry Festival was over. They were ready to search the middle of Lake Sanford for a bag that may have been tossed from a rowboat. The pilot drove the boat to the middle of the lake in view of Mrs. Albers' window, where she could clearly see it.

The divers knew they were trying to find a needle in a haystack because they didn't know exactly where the suspicious bag was dropped into the lake. The lake was not as muddy as many inland lakes, so the chances of finding something fairly large were better than average. Divers went down one at a time, and each came back empty-handed.

Each went down again in another area, and again found nothing. The crew didn't have a sonar device, so it was really a case of hunt and hope to find something on the lake bottom. The divers went down a third time, but after several minutes, they returned without the bag they sought.

After three dives with nothing to show for them, the pilot received a message that the crew was needed at a nearby lake where a possible drowning had occurred. They notified Detective Morrison and quickly vacated the area, planning to file a report later in the day.

⹂❀⹁

On his way to Traverse City, Lou pulled into a rest area. He called Jack, asking him to go to Greenville and learn what he could about Joanne Tuttle. "I'll get right on it, Lou."

Jack checked his computer at www.whitepages.com for an address and phone number. There was only one address for a Tuttle in Greenville. That number was listed under 'Steve,' with a 'Joanne' living at the residence.

Jack bade Elaine farewell and headed for Greenville, 40 or so miles to the east of Muskegon. No one was home at the Tuttle address, and nobody answered the phone. But Lou had said Joanne could be Catholic, so Jack drove to the Catholic church and asked the secretary if she knew whether Joanne Tuttle was employed, and if so, where.

The receptionist was reluctant to give out any information, but when Jack explained that he was an investigator, she responded, "She works at Carl's Tire Service." Jack thanked her, entered the business name into his car's GPS, and saw that he was only a few blocks away.

At Carl's Tire Service, a woman worked at a computer in a small office. "Excuse me. Might you be Joanne Tuttle?"

"Yes. One of the service representatives will be with you in a minute or two."

"Thanks, but I came to see *you*."

"Salesmen should talk to Carl, the owner."

"I'm not a salesman. I'm assisting the Traverse City police in the murder of your ex-husband. Could I ask you some questions?"

Joanne's manner turned cold. "Well, I'm on the clock right now."

"As I said, I'd like to ask you some questions. I don't consider you a suspect, but as someone who might have information that would help us."

"I can talk with you for a few minutes when I get off for lunch. The boss doesn't like me taking time for personal matters. Besides, I have nothing to say about Tom's murder."

"When will that be?"

"Noon, and not a minute before."

"I'll be back then. Thank you."

Jack turned and walked out, passing a man he assumed was Carl, who marched right into Joanne's office. "Who was *that* guy?"

"He's working with a detective looking into Tom's murder."

"You didn't *tell* him anything, did you?"

"Of course not! He said I wasn't a suspect, but I might have information that would help in the investigation. He's coming back at noon."

Glancing at his watch Jack knew he had an hour till he could talk to Joanne. He walked along Lafayette Street and went into the Robbin's Booklist. Bookstores just drew him in. On one wall was a poster advertising Greenville's Danish Festival in August. That sounded like fun, and he hoped he and Elaine could come over for the festivities.

Still with time on his hands, Jack sought out the public library. Here he could read newspapers or the latest magazines and, more important on this hot day, relax in an air-conditioned building. On a school day, he could have gone to Greenville High School in hopes of seeing Lou's teaching friend, Kim Bell. Kim often read a portion of Lou's books to her students each day.

Jack signed up for time at a library computer. He typed "Tuttle" in the 'search' box of the *Greenville News*. He had no idea of what might appear, but a few articles popped up.

The first one had the headline,

Local NRA President Urges Women to Carry Guns for Safety.

Jack read on,

> *Joanne Tuttle, local chapter president, issued a press release urging women in Greenville to register a firearm and take a one-week course in gun safety. Tuttle said, 'You never know when your security or safety will be threatened. It's better to be safe than sorry.'*

The second article was a letter to the editor. It read,

Gun control is getting too much press. Just because some innocent people die by gunshots is not a reason to prohibit citizens from having guns. I urge everyone who believes in the First Amendment to write to their congressmen, state legislators, county, and local politicians. Tell them to get off your back. Gun ownership is protected by the Constitution. Stand up and be counted.

— *J. Tuttle, Greenville.*

There were only a couple more references, one for a bowling score, and the other an announcement of those chosen for a Grand Rapids roller derby team. Joanne Tuttle, "The Bruiser," had been voted team co-captain.

⚜❋⚜

As predicted, Lou arrived in Traverse City about noon. Lou got into Rod Morrison's vehicle, and they drove to the Northernmost Winery to serve the search warrant. When they arrived they met the maintenance worker, Stone Elliott, and informed him of the warrant. They were pleased to find an employee on-site, so no damage need be done by forcibly entering a building or office. Stone was told he was not to go into the offices, but the detective would alert him when they were finished.

The first items confiscated were the computers: Tom's, Christy's and the finance manager's. Lou looked at the short stack of messages on Tom's desk. Most were from Christy, but one jumped out as possibly relevant. It read, "Please call Corky about cancelled order." The phone number on the message was out-of-state.

Detective Morrison looked over the recent mail and found nothing of interest. He also looked at the 'to be filed' basket and saw a file labeled, 'California Contacts.' It contained orders for grapes, and in most of them, they had been grown in Napa, California. There were several lading forms in the folder indicating dates of delivery and the names of shipping companies. Lou confiscated this paperwork in case they needed to contact the shippers.

The detectives located Stone and explained that they were leaving. Lou said to Stone, "Thank you for talking with Jack Kelly last evening at the funeral home. We appreciate your help." Stone nodded with a weak smile.

"Ah, Mr. Searing could I have a word with you?"

"Certainly." Detective Morrison walked to his cruiser leaving Lou and Stone to talk.

"Christy is gone."

"You mean today, from work?"

"I mean she's *gone,* for good."

"Do you mean dead, quit her job, or moved from the area?"

"I know she's not in the area, and I expect she'll die."

"Why?" asked Lou, surprised. "Do you know, or have a theory?"

"She owes someone a lot of money, and she doesn't have it, and she can't get it."

"She *told* you this?" Lou asked.

"The woman she fired, our former brew master, Heather Adams, told me. She asked me to keep the fact to myself, but I want to help solve Tom's murder."

"I appreciate your telling me. Do you know where Christy is now?"

"No. I got the impression she might be out of the country."

"You heard this from the brew master. Do you think Heather is the reason Christy left the area? Or do you think she just heard something and wanted to share it with you?"

"I don't know why she chose to tell me."

"Christy fired Heather, right?" Lou asked.

"Yeah."

"The logical question is, do you think Heather has threatened Christy? Or, is Christy involved with Tom McNutt's murder?"

"I don't know, but I certainly wouldn't rule out Christy as a suspect."

"Thanks, Stone, I much appreciate your help," Lou said, shaking his hand. He turned and walked to the police car.

⚘

Meanwhile in Greenville, Jack headed for the tire store to meet Joanne. She walked out of the store at noon and came over to Jack, who was standing beside his car. "Okay, you said you had a few questions. Let's get this over with so I can get some lunch."

"For the record, you were married to Tom McNutt. Is that true?"

"Yes."

"Are you surprised that Tom was murdered?"

"No."

"Do you have any idea who may have shot him?"

"I don't know, but I have a hunch or two."

"Will you share those hunches?"

"My first guess would be someone in his company. He hires and fires at a moment's notice. My second guess would be someone who lost to him."

"Lost to him?" Jack asked, seeking clarification.

"Yeah, second place in the contest for Grand Marshal, second place in one of his ocean sailing races, second place in a wine-selling contest. You may not know this, but Tom had an arrogant side. He was cocky, in love with himself, and always better than the next guy. He would rub in any victory till those who didn't win would become furious."

"I see. We haven't heard that he was arrogant."

"It seems in investigating a crime like this, you not only need the killer, but you also need the personality of the victim.

What causes someone to kill and risk life in prison? It has to be a pretty strong reason."

"You and Tom divorced, correct?" Jack asked.

"It's none of your business what the status of our marriage is, but as far as the church is concerned, we are married."

"I see. You need an annulment to have your current marriage recognized by the church. Am I right?"

"That's right and that's where Tom was at his worst. He wouldn't cooperate. He befriended Father Pat, who advised him how he should act to be sure the Diocesan Tribunal never brought my annulment request up for decision."

"Why would Tom care if an annulment went through or not?"

"It was a way to punish me, which he did all the time we were married. He was a control freak, and this was one way he could still control me every day of my life."

"As I recall Catholic procedures, for a marriage to be invalidated, either you need an annulment, or one of the partners must have died."

"Yes," Joanne replied, and taking a deep breath added, "And, now I become a suspect."

"Not necessarily," Jack replied. "So, if you didn't kill him or arrange the murder, you must be pretty relieved to have him dead now."

"Boy, you got that right!"

"I understand you are a strong firearms proponent," Jack remarked off-handedly.

"How would you know that?" Joanne asked, surprised at his comment.

"I do research, and I take my role as Mr. Searing's assistant seriously. I also know you are a leader. You are President of the local NRA Chapter and the captain of your roller derby team."

"Not much gets past you."

"That's my job. Thank you for talking with me. Enjoy your lunch."

"You're welcome." Jack watched Joanne walk to her car. He noted that it was a blue Ford Focus, and he took a photo of it with his Smart Phone. He wanted to see if a similar car had been in the funeral home parking lot, or if Sara's photo was of the same vehicle.

⁂

Lou was to contact Corky and see what he could learn. He dialed the number written on the post-it note.

"Hello," Corky said, looking at his caller ID. "Lou Searing, whoever and wherever you are. What can I do for you?"

"Can I assume this is Corky?"

"You got the cork dork. Got an order?"

"No, I'm not in the wine business."

"Then why did you call me, Lou Searing? If you're selling something, I've got too much of it at the moment. If you want information, you're out of luck. If you're a solicitor wanting money, my list of charities is short, and you're not on it."

"None of the above. I'm investigating the murder of Tom McNutt, and I'd like to ask you a few questions."

"Tom's dead? Did I hear right?"

"He was killed a few days ago at the Cherry Festival in Traverse City."

"Well, *I* didn't do it, if that's one of your questions. But I'll bet you've a long list of suspects."

"We don't have a *long* list. Should we?" Lou asked, surprised at the comment.

"Anyone with millions has clout. When a man has clout, he deals with people who don't. That creates conflict which can or can't be resolved. When it can't, you have potential for poor judgment. There are people in every realm of Tom's life who resent his money and power, and who use poor judgment. You need to find the one person who went over the edge."

"Do you know who that might be?"

"His brew master, Heather Adams; his manager, Christy Johnson; his former wife, Joanne Tuttle; his current wife, Martha; his fellow winery-owners; or a hit man for one of the above."

"Hmmm, that's quite a list," Lou replied. "I was under the impression that he didn't have enemies. Everybody loved him."

"Well, you've evidence that one didn't. Correct?" Corky asked.

"Obviously. With all due respect, I asked if you knew who the murderer might be. I didn't ask for suspects, though everyone you mention is on my list."

"The answer to your question is a tie between Tom's first wife and me."

"You?" Lou asked.

"Tom McNutt ruined my career. He was instrumental in convincing several winery owners to break their contracts with my company. For years I have supplied excellent corks and outstanding service to Tom and his winery friends. Losing those contracts devastated my company. It caused layoffs, huge cuts in pay for me and other salesmen. Of course, I wanted him to pay for ruining so many lives. It's karma. You destroy the livelihood of people, your livelihood will be destroyed. And it was."

"It sounds like you're admitting to killing him."

"It does, but one ingredient is missing.'

"What's that?" Lou asked.

"I'm intelligent. Meaning, my desire to kill him led to the question of how I wanted to spend my time on Earth. In prison with a bunch of losers was not the answer. I decided to sit back and let someone with less intelligence do the job for me."

"And that's what happened?"

"Correct. Tom and I worked together since he was hired at a winery in Wisconsin. Over the years we've shared a lot of wine and conversation, much of it personal. Friends do that, including friends who are business associates. You learn a lot."

"Yes, I'll bet you do."

"Tom got himself involved with a woman who didn't love him, but she loved his social contacts, parties, and charity balls. You can finish the story."

"I don't know much about her," Lou admitted.

"You should make it your business to learn all you can."

"I know her name and where she lives," Lou replied. "I'll make her a priority."

"Makes sense."

"Let me ask you one more question," Lou said. "A thirteen year-old girl saw a female suspect lose a wine cork. Does this mean anything to you?"

"It indicates a wine-drinker who wants to dispose of it appropriately. It means she's a collector. It means she has a friend who collects corks."

"Common sense, but that's what I needed to hear. Thanks for talking with me, Corky."

"I'm sorry Tom has died. He was a good man, but I'm not surprised. Several people are breathing a little easier, I can assure you."

⊰❀⊱

While he was in Traverse City, one of Lou's goals was to talk with the brew master, Heather Adams.

Lou found an address for Heather in Sutton's Bay, a small community up the west arm of Grand Traverse Bay. He drove to the address, only to find no one home. A man next door who was mowing his lawn killed the mower's engine and shouted to get Lou's attention.

"There's nobody home!"

"Does Heather live here?" Lou shouted back.

"They're on vacation!"

"Heather and her family?"

"Just Heather and her live-in friend."

"Do you know where they went?"

"No!"

"Do you know when they'll be back?"

"No!"

"Thanks!" Lou said, turning to leave. Just then a car pulled in behind his car, and a woman got out and approached Lou.

"Are you looking for Heather or Dennis?"

"Either one, actually. Do you know where I can find them?"

"Why are you looking for them?" the woman asked.

"I want to ask some questions. Who are you, by the way?" Lou asked.

"That's *my* question for *you*," the stranger replied.

"I'm Lou Searing, and I'm assisting the Traverse City police investigating the murder of Tom McNutt, Heather's former boss. I'm hoping she might be able to help me."

"I'm Tammy Baumer. I'm brew master at another winery on the peninsula. We're friends, and I'm watching her place while she's on vacation."

"Do you know where she went on vacation?"

"Yes, but I won't tell you. She's under a lot of stress and needs time away. The last thing I'd do is send you to her to add even more stress."

"That's kind of you, but I don't think you'd want to withhold information. There are harsh penalties for that."

"I don't care! You can see her when she comes home!"

"When will that be?" Lou asked.

"A couple of weeks."

"Much too long. Listen, she is not a suspect—I just want to ask a few questions. Why don't you call her, explain who I am and what I need, and ask her to call me. I really don't think I'll add to her stress—unless she's running from the authorities."

"I assure you, she is *not running* from anything and is *not* involved in a murder. She had nothing good to say about her boss, but she wouldn't kill him."

"Then, why not answer a couple of questions?" Lou asked, confused as to why he was being rebuffed.

"I'll call her and explain what you want. If she wants to talk to you, she can call you."

"Fine. I don't mean to sound difficult, but if she doesn't call, we might have to get a warrant to find her. So, if she wants to avoid stress, I suggest she call me."

"I understand."

"By the way, who is Dennis?"

"He's a friend. They worked together at the winery."

"Where is he?"

"He's with Heather."

"I think there was another person let go at the same time, an Anthony Kellogg?"

"He's with her, too."

"Really."

"They're all bummed out over being fired, and they're sort of supporting each other during this stressful time."

"I see. Well, please make your phone call, and I'll wait to hear from them."

The two parted, Lou wondering when he would hear from Heather.

ॐ❀ॐ

Lou's cell phone rang before he left Sutton's Bay. Caller ID read Heather Adams.

"Hi. Heather?"

"Yes, Mr. Searing. I'm sorry I wasn't at home to talk with you. Tammy explained what you wanted. What questions do you have?"

"Tammy probably told you I'm assisting in the murder investigation of your former boss."

"I'm so sorry to hear that Tom was killed. He was a fine man, and the community has lost a wonderful citizen."

"I thought you'd be bitter because he let you go."

"Oh, no, he did what he had to do. We brew masters are unique, and we work at the pleasure of the winery owner. We bounce around like tennis balls, hoping to find a good match between what we produce and what the winery owner wants. I'll have another job soon. In fact, I'm on my way to an interview in Wisconsin. We're calling it a vacation, too."

"I see. I have questions."

"Sure. I'm happy to help."

"When you make wine at a winery, do you use only grapes that you grow in your vineyards?"

"No. Most wineries supplement their grapes with some shipped in from other vineyards."

"I thought that was illegal," Lou replied.

"It is only illegal if the label implies that *all* the grapes are grown at the winery."

"Is it illegal or unethical to have wine produced in, let's say, California, shipped here, bottled in Michigan, carrying a label indicating it is Michigan wine?"

"For sure!"

"Did you do this at Tom's winery?"

"Yes." Heather sounded subdued.

"So, Tom knew he was violating the law by bringing in California-produced wine and labeling it as Michigan wine."

"Of *course* he knew it."

"Did you object?"

"Yes, I *did,* and that was probably part of the reason I am no longer on his staff."

"But the wine sold very well, or so I'm told," Lou said.

"Well, that's due in part to Tom's reputation. I was often embarrassed by the quality of the wine we bottled, but Tom's the boss, and we did what he said."

"So, in a sense, it's a relief not to work for Tom."

"Definitely. In fact, I didn't even list Tom's winery on my resume. I'll tell a prospective winery owner of my work experience, but I'm not proud to say that part of my career was working at the Northernmost Winery."

"Dennis and Anthony were let go as well, right?" Lou asked.

"Now that's another matter," Heather said, her voice becoming angry. "That was a big mistake. Denny and Tony made that winery successful."

"How are *they* handling this?" Lou asked.

"Not well. They'll have trouble finding work. They're angry and bitter, and I'm concerned for them. I suggested they come with me to Wisconsin because I thought getting out of town would be a good break."

"Is their bitterness and anger such that *they* may have killed Tom?"

"I would say, 'yes,' but neither of them have said a word about it."

"Do you know if either of them knows a Joanne Tuttle?"

"I don't know. You'd need to talk to them about that."

"Are they there with you?" Lou asked.

"Yes. I'll put Denny on. If we don't talk after you speak with Denny, call me anytime. I'm willing to help you."

"Thank you. Tammy gave me the impression that I would find you upset."

"That's Tammy—sort of a mother-hen type. She can be difficult at times. So, you call me whenever you need to."

"Thanks, Heather. Please put Denny on."

"Okay, here he is."

"Hello, Mr. Searing."

"Thanks for talking with me, Denny. It must be quite disheartening to be let go at the winery."

"Thank you. I've never been unemployed before, so it's difficult for me. You had some questions?"

"Yes. Did you know Joanne Tuttle in Greenville?"

"Yes, she was Mr. McNutt's first wife."

"Do you think she killed Tom?"

"She's who I'd put *my* money on."

"Would she do it herself or hire it done?"

"Hire it."

"I see. Did she hire *you* to do it?" Lou asked.

"She asked me about it, but I sure didn't want to live my life in prison."

"But, she did talk to you about the possibility."

"Yes, she did."

"Do you know who might have said yes?"

"Christy."

"Christy Johnson?"

"That'd be my guess. Either her or someone in Joanne's NRA Chapter."

"How about Anthony? Would he have any more details for me?"

"I don't think so. He's a quiet guy who keeps to himself. I'm not even sure he knows Tom is dead."

"Thanks for your information, Denny. Please thank Heather again for me."

"Will do. Good-bye."

Lou disconnected, then called Stone Elliott.

"Yes, Mr. Searing. What can I do for you?"

"I need a photo of the people who worked at the winery this past year, especially Christy, Heather, Denny, and Anthony. Are there any group photos of workers, maybe from a holiday party or a staff picnic?"

"There are photos in the annual report. And, if you go to our website, you'll find employee photos there."

"I'll do that. Thanks!"

✿❀✿

Jack had a hunch Lou needed him, so he called Elaine from Greenville to explain that he was going on to Traverse City. It was perfect timing, because Lou asked him to review their auto photos in hopes that two would match and make sense of who was where. First Jack analyzed the Mackinac Bridge videos, noting all plate information as well as make of car, and whenever possible counting the number of people in the vehicle.

In the meantime, Lou was concerned with Christy Johnson. Where was she and what role, if any, did she play in the murder? His cell phone rang, showing Chief Bixler's ID.

"Well, Lou, do you need more drama in this case?"

"What do you have for us?" Lou asked.

"A bomb went off at the Northernmost Winery, totally destroying the winery offices. Thankfully, no one was in the building at the time. It was closed off because of our search warrant, but had Christy Johnson been in her office, she'd be dead right now."

"Hmmm."

"The search warrant is useless since the place was literally blown to smithereens."

"Nobody called in as a witness or to claim responsibility?" Lou asked.

"No."

"The longer this case takes, the larger part Christy seems to play in the story," Lou reasoned.

"Maybe someone is seeking revenge for her killing McNutt," Stacy Bixler replied.

"Or, maybe someone wants to keep us away from something incriminating."

"Either could be the case," Lou replied.

"Well, that's it, Lou. I'm just keeping you up-to-date."

"Thanks very much, Chief."

✣❀✣

In a Traverse City Police Department conference room, Jack sat before a table with all the photos of cars and license plates, engrossed in a match-to-sample activity. In less than five minutes, he found a match. The photo of Joanne Tuttle's car in Greenville was like a vehicle in the funeral home parking lot. A few minutes later he spotted another match. A car going through the Mackinac Bridge toll gate matched one of Jack's photos taken on a trip to Sanford Lake.

⭐

Jack called Lou and Rod Morrison to the conference room to go over his auto matches. "What have you got for us, Jack?" Lou asked.

"I found some interesting matches. I'll give you the match, and you try to make sense of it."

Lou and Rod perused the photos arranged on the table. "Okay. Give us match number one," Rod said to Jack.

"This car is owned by Tom McNutt's ex-wife, Joanne Tuttle, who lives in Greenville. But, I don't see this car in the Mackinac Bridge videos."

"What's your second match?" Lou asked.

"I saved the best for last. When Lou told me about a boat on Sanford Lake, I decided to drive slowly around the lake, taking photos of as many cars as I could without treading on private property. This is my best effort at helping us. These two match." Jack pointed to a photo of a yellow Buick parked by a cabin on the lake, then pointed out an identical car waiting to go through the toll gate at the Bridge.

"Hmmm, this could be significant," Lou said. "But it's based on a number of unproven assumptions."

"Right," Rod replied. "We have no proof anyone at Sanford Lake is involved in the murder. We're not sure that what was dropped overboard is in fact associated with the murder, or that the person who dropped something overboard is associated with this car."

"And, to top it all off, our information comes from a blind woman who sits in an imaginary lighthouse and logs what she sees," Rod said, shaking his head.

Lou thought for a moment. "Well, I'm no statistician, but the odds of a vehicle in a traffic jam at the Bridge matching a car seen in the Traverse City area hours earlier, with the occupants of both cars not involved in this kidnapping are awfully slim.

"Wait a minute," Jack interjected. "I almost forgot. When we went to the wineries, I took photos of cars there, but I didn't include them in this analysis. Give me a few minutes to do that."

Lou and Detective Morrison left the room to check messages on their cell phones. When they returned, Jack had interesting news.

"Look at this. The yellow car belongs to Christy. See it here in the Northernmost Winery parking lot? Now look at the Bridge video. The same vehicle appears behind the pickup truck. See it?"

Lou remarked dryly. "This doesn't look good for Christy Johnson."

Detective Morrison was quick to add, "But, we don't know that she's in that car."

"I stand corrected," Lou admitted. "But we need to find Christy Johnson. If she's not our murderer, she still needs to explain why her car was parked at the funeral home if she didn't go in. And why was she part of a kidnapping at the Mackinac Bridge?"

"If she is the murderer, who's the accomplice?" Jack asked. "Who drove her car from the gas station to the county park where the motor home was left? Who was with her in the car after Sara was taken? Was someone with her at the cabin on Sanford Lake?"

"So we've at least two people to account for in this case, maybe more."

"I'm fairly certain Christy is one of them, but who's the other?" Rod asked. "Her husband?"

"Always the first suspect," Lou said. "Let's get a bead on him as well."

❦

Late in the afternoon, Cherry Festival Director Jerry Waters got in touch with Lou. "I talked to Chief Bixler, trying to follow protocol, but she told me to talk to you."

"What do you have for me, Jerry? By the way, are you sleeping better now that this year's festival is in the history books?"

"There's a lot of follow-up work to be done. Actually I'm busier than when the festival was in full swing. Anyway, the reason for my call is that I heard from a high school student, Tim Jacobs, who was a member of the Traverse City Central High School marching band. He wasn't in formation since musicians and others were free to hang around the set-up area until they needed to march. He saw someone come out of the queen's float entrance to the pickup while people were scattering after the gunshot or going up to see the body."

"Hmmm, that's interesting."

"He didn't want to say anything because of Sara's trouble but in church last Sunday, something changed his mind."

"That's good. Did he know the person who he saw coming out?"

"He doesn't know the person, but he does remember something that might help."

"And that is?"

"The person was a man disguised as a woman."

"We figured that might have happened," Lou said, smiling and clapping his hands once.

"But there's more," Jerry offered.

"Tim saw a large, shiny ring on one of this man's fingers. The sun must have hit it just right. He probably couldn't identify the guy in a line-up, but he'll not forget that ring."

"Guy?" Lou said, surprised to hear the new information. "I thought we were targeting a woman?"

"He said, 'a guy.' That's all I can tell you," Jerry replied.

"Thanks for the information. Please thank young Jacobs, and tell him that if he remembers anything else, he shouldn't hesitate to call me."

"I'll do that, Lou."

Lou shared what he had just learned with the others.

"Whoever he is, a large ring heightens the chances that he's wealthy," Jack said.

"That is, if it's a diamond. It could be glass," Detective Morrison replied.

"I'll bet you're good with crossword puzzles," Lou said. "You see every side to an issue."

"That's why he's a detective, Lou," Jack said, with a chuckle. "It takes a special mind to think differently than most."

"I know that. I was thinking the same thing, but Rod just happened to blurt it out before I could get a word in edgewise."

"Nice try, Lou," Jack said with a smile.

"Just thinking on my feet, Jack. A few grey cells up in the noggin still fire on occasion."

"Oh, I know they do."

"Let's call it a day. Anything we need to do can wait till tomorrow," Lou said. The day's work was complete, but the case had still not been solved.

Lou and Jack got rooms at a Comfort Inn, and the two men agreed to meet for the continental breakfast at 8:00 a.m.

Lou called Carol to see how her day was and to report on developments. This would have been the perfect evening for a walk on the beach, and they both missed the opportunity.

Jack called Elaine and they discussed their day's activities and plans for tomorrow. Jack planned to watch *CSI* because he could never get enough ideas, and he liked to try to solve the case before the characters did. Lou, on the other hand, had had enough crime investigation for the day. He turned on the Tigers and watched Verlander win another game, putting the Tigers six games up in the American League Central Division.

CHAPTER EIGHT

Day 5 • July 10

Lou and Jack decided that they would head home after a day of work. Lou wanted to relax, and Jack thought he had done all that Lou had asked of him.

As Lou checked out, he got a cell phone call from Stone Elliott at the Northernmost Winery. "I need to talk to you, and it needs to be somewhere that is a bit isolated."

"OK, we can do that. Name a place."

"A breakwater juts out into the Bay downtown, near the city zoo. I don't want us to walk out there together. You walk to the end. Then I'll check whether anyone is in the vicinity who knows me or could connect me to the winery. If I think the coast is clear, we can talk. If not, I'll simply head back to the shore, get into my car, and leave, and we'll make other arrangements later. Understood?"

"Understood. Do you mind if Jack comes along?"

"I'd rather he not join us on the breakwater," Stone replied.

"I think I'll ask him to watch from a distance," Lou replied. "I'll brief him later. I can be there by 9:30. Will that work for you?"

"Yes. See you soon."

Lou explained to Jack that he was meeting Stone on the breakwater. Jack was to watch the two conversing from the shore and pick up on any suspicious activity or people watching while they talked.

At 9:30 Lou stood at the end of the breakwater, watching waves lap up on the cement. Two fishermen a little closer to shore seemed engrossed in an attempt to take home dinner. Whenever Lou looked to see if Stone was approaching, he saw no one. He wondered if his time was wrong; there must be a good reason for Stone being late. Lou decided simply to wait.

At ten o'clock, Stone still had not appeared, and Lou had no messages on his phone. At five after ten Lou saw two men in suits walking in his direction. They weren't coming to fish, and they walked as if they had a mission. Lou's heart started to beat harder as he thought about being overtaken, killed, or thrown into the Bay. *What chance would an unarmed man have against two younger and stronger men?* Lou thought.

As Lou turned to look at the Bay rather than at the two men, he saw Jack fall in behind them, keeping about 10 yards behind. He noticed that they were not talking to each other. They weren't on the breakwater for exercise, and they didn't appear to be friends out for a walk. Jack tried to decide what he would do if Lou were threatened. One thing he *could* do was take a photo behind the men, which he did.

The two men walked up to Lou, each standing to one side. Lou said, "Nice morning for a walk."

"Yes, it is."

There was a moment of silence as the three looked over the Bay. Jack stayed relatively close and spoke with the fishermen to offer grounds for his presence on the breakwater.

Lou turned and looked back toward shore. He found some comfort in seeing Jack nearby, even though he didn't know what help Jack could be in the event of a problem. He also spotted Stone getting out of his car and walking toward him. Neither man said a word to Lou.

As Stone approached, he was disturbed to see Jack fairly close to Lou, Stone walked up to the three men and stood to the right of Lou while the two younger men turned to face the shore.

"Sorry I'm late. It couldn't be helped."

"No problem. Are these two guys with you?" Lou asked.

"Yes. They're protecting us. I thought it was clear that Jack wasn't to be out here."

"It was clear, but you weren't here, and your strongmen looked ominous coming toward me. Jack was simply being protective and came out this way."

"I understand."

"What do you have for me, and why all of this secrecy?" Lou asked.

"That will become clear. I trust you didn't tell the police about our meeting?"

"Of course not."

"Good."

Stone took a deep breath before he spoke. "I got a call last night from Christy. She gave me information, but also a clear and strong message not to repeat a word of what she told me. I gave her my word, and I don't mind telling you that I feel guilty passing it on to you. However, I was raised to help others, and though I'm betraying Christy, I believe that in the long run, telling you what I heard is best."

"Thank you for taking me into your confidence," Lou said.

"As I said, I got a call from Christy. She's coming from Wisconsin on the Badger ferry, arriving in Ludington around six this evening. She is not alone, but I don't know who the other person is."

"Interesting. She's coming from Wisconsin."

"I'll explain later. What you need to know is that you are a target and your death is slated for tonight."

"Well, that *is* a bit disheartening. I've received threats before. They haven't materialized, so I don't take them seriously. But at the same time, I don't brush them off."

"This isn't one to take lightly. You're now a big threat. She knows you have a witness, the teenage girl who took photos, and who may be able to pick Christy out of a lineup. She knows the girl found a cork, which lead the police to our winery. She knows you are on the case. And in her own words, 'He's solved a dozen murders in Michigan, and chances are good he'll get me too.' She knows you had a search warrant for the offices, and she knows the office building was bombed. So, either you implicate her in the murder, or she kills you. I hope you don't ever tell her you heard this from me, or I'll be soon be dead."

"I am eternally grateful, Mr. Elliott. She didn't tell you where or how I'm to be killed? I assume you would have told me."

"That's right. She may have people tracking you, I don't know. She didn't say how she knows where you are, but I assume someone will keep her informed."

"The challenge now is to outsmart her," Lou replied. "Not only her, but unknown persons keeping eyes on me."

"I could be in trouble too, because for all I know, we're being watched right now, and Christy will be informed of this conversation. That's why I brought a couple of body guards with me, just in case her guys want me, you, or *us* taken someplace for an execution."

"It all makes sense now," Lou said. "You're taking a huge risk on my behalf, and as I said, I'm grateful."

"I'm praying with all my heart, mind, and soul that you *do* outsmart her. She is like a caged tiger, bent on taking you out because she sees you as her nemesis."

"Hopefully, once she's behind bars, you and I can share a cup of coffee or a meal while we take a deep breath."

"Good luck, Lou."

"Thank you, Stone." The two body guards walked together back to the lot. Lou, Stone, and Jack went back to the beach at different times, each hoping that no one was watching them.

※ ❀ ※

Lou knew he had several hours before Christy would try to kill him. The Badger would arrive in Ludington early in the evening, and then there was the drive to Traverse City. Lou figured he had until at least 8:00 to craft a plan.

Lou asked Jack, Detective Morrison, and Police Chief Bixler to meet him at the police station at noon. He felt like he was ordering his last meal, and for the first time in forever, he realized he didn't need to give any thought to what he ate. If he were in Lansing, he would order a burger, fries, and a chocolate malt from *Johnny Rockets*. But, if he lived, as he fully intended he would, it would behoove him to order something healthy. He asked Jack to bring some lunch with him; Jack was to decide what comprised a healthy meal, not Lou. He chose tuna sandwiches, chips, and Diet Cokes.

The four sat in a conference room at the police station, exchanging small talk while they ate lunch. As the meal finished, Lou began. "This morning I was offered a major tip in the McNutt murder investigation. In fact, the case could be wrapped up by sunset."

That comment got everyone's attention. "You sure know how to open a meeting, Lou," Police Chief Bixler remarked.

"Specifically, Christy Johnson is coming after *me,* because she thinks that I'm in the way of her safe escape."

"How do you know this, Lou?" Jack asked.

"Stone Elliott has turned on Christy and others and is now an informant working with us."

"Then we need to get you hidden away, Lou," Detective Morrison said in a serious tone of voice.

"Definitely," Bixler replied. "You're sleeping in jail tonight, Lou. The accommodations aren't great, but we guarantee you'll wake up in the morning." Everyone chuckled nervously.

"What do you need me to do, Lou?" Jack asked.

"I want you to go home, and not a word to Carol. This news would probably give her a heart attack, and it would end my career as an investigator. She'd fit me with a nose-ring on a heavy chain tied around her waist."

"I won't say a word to Elaine or Carol, but I'm not going home. My job is to be your assistant, and I don't turn tail and run when a threat is made. Especially when it's a death threat."

"I appreciate that, but we don't know what Christy has planned. I don't mind being in harm's way—it comes with the territory. But I want you safely out of the way, Jack, because this case isn't worth your life as well. So, please do as I say, and leave after this meeting."

"I can't do it, Lou," Jack replied. "We'll talk later."

"Then let's talk about strategy," Lou continued. "Stone has told me that Christy is crossing on the Badger, due to arrive in Ludington during the dinner hour. She'll come on to Traverse City, so we need to be ready about 8:00 p.m."

"Yes, if you assume she's coming by car," Detective Morrison reminded them. "She could fly, for all we know. Also, while I have the floor, if she's coming to Traverse City to kill you, someone must have told her you are here. That someone has to know where you are right now, and this person or persons will monitor your movements till Christy arrives.

"There's another assumption we can't make," Detective Morrison continued. "We may expect Christy to try to kill Lou, but it could be someone else acting on her behalf. So, we don't have till eight o'clock. The murder could be planned for any time."

Chief Bixler spoke up. "One thing is for certain: we can monitor Christy's movements. From the moment she walks off the Badger in Ludington, she'll be a marked woman, and we'll know where she is every minute, as well as who's with her."

"Those are good points," Lou said. "This is why we needed a meeting of the minds."

"So we have a plan that involves two forces, Lou and Christy, and the goal is for their paths not to meet," Chief Bixler summarized.

"Exactly," Jack replied. "As humorous as it was, I liked the idea of Lou locked up in jail. That seems like a pretty safe place to be."

"Unless we feel comfortable using Lou as a carrot," Chief Bixler replied.

"A carrot?" Jack asked.

"We could have your informant tell Christy that he heard Lou would be wherever we decide on, and then we'd fortify the place. We'd cover it like a blanket with plainclothes officers from the sheriff's office, my staff, and the state police."

"You mean like staying at a certain motel?" Jack asked. "But in reality he'd be far away, right?"

"No, Lou would have to literally walk into the motel. We would need to catch Christy or her accomplice in the attempt to kill him."

"No innkeeper will allow that. Everyone would panic and the place will get a bad reputation."

"Good point," Lou said. "Maybe I need to be on her turf, like at the Northernmost Winery. It's isolated and nobody's around. The informant could tell Christy I'm working at the winery because I've found some leads."

"I like that," Chief Bixler replied. "We'll follow you out to the winery in unmarked cars, and we'll already have officers on site, out of view."

"Sounds good," Lou said, pleased that the others liked his idea. "How will I be a target at the winery?"

"That will take some thought," Chief Bixler realized. "We want Christy or the hit man to do something to warrant an arrest. It can't be trespassing, because she has every right to be on the property. The best thing might be to have her see a shadow in a window, which she could assume would be Lou. In reality it would be cardboard, or a dummy."

Jack asked Stacy. "Would a clothing store loan you a mannequin, a bald mannequin?"

"Oh, sure. Zeb Horvath would work with me. Replacing a plastic model would not be a problem if that is necessary."

"Okay," Jack said and continued, "we put a mannequin where it would be visible, with its back to the window, or if she uses the door, she would see the back of Lou. I mean the mannequin. If she falls for it, takes a shot at the dummy, your officers move in and make the arrest."

"Let's make sure there aren't any holes in this," Detective Morrison said, "lest we overlook something important."

"So, we don't stop her when she gets off the Badger or while she is *en route* to Traverse City," Lou began to summarize.

Chief Bixler finished explaining the plan. "Yes, let her move as she wishes. Just have the informant let her know that Lou will be at the winery this evening, probably in the tasting room, studying office records. The explosion destroyed everything but the tasting room. We'll be hidden around the winery, and if she shoots, we'll arrest her. Lou and Jack must stay out of sight, because we don't know exactly who's looking for them. For all we know, someone might know Lou and Jack are here in the station and could report that to Christy. Christy might be confused whether to listen to the stake-out person or the informant."

"That's easy enough," Lou responded. "Have Stone tell her that Jack and I were here, but we left in disguise without being seen. And I think I can solve the case by checking records I'm convinced are in the tasting room."

"Good. I like that," Detective Morrison replied.

"So, Jack and I have to stay here till this all plays out?" Lou asked.

"Hey, what's to complain about?" Chief Bixler asked, in a light tone of voice. "You'll have television, weights, cards and a cot. It's not exactly the Holiday Inn, but for seven hours it's habitable."

Chief Bixler left them with, "Make yourselves at home, guys. I'll even tell the cook you can have access to the kitchen cupboards." She and Detective Morrison went about their work, leaving Lou and Jack in the conference room.

.⚚.

Lou and Jack had some quiet time to reflect.

"Well, this is not how I expected this to go," Lou said. "I figured Joanne Tuttle was behind the murder."

"So did I. With McNutt out of the way, she can marry in the church."

"But, is that really a big enough issue to kill someone over?" Lou mused.

"You tell me," Jack replied. "You're Catholic."

"I would say 'definitely not,' but each person sees the world differently. That might only be one factor in the equation. Who knows what motivation she could have?"

"For a while I thought the brew master and the other two workers may have wanted revenge for their being fired, but Heather sounded very matter-of-fact about it, and confident that they would find jobs."

Lou's cell phone rang; the display indicated it was Carol. "Excuse me, Jack. I need to take it."

"Absolutely,"

"Hi, Sweetzie," Lou used one of his few endearing pet names for Carol.

"Hi, just wondering if you'll be home this evening. It'll be a nice evening for a walk on the beach."

"Let's move that walk ahead 24 hours. We're very close to solving this case. We've got a good lead, and we hope to make an arrest tonight. I can't leave right now."

"That's fine. I understand. I just had my fingers crossed that you would be home. I even made a batch of chocolate chip cookies."

"Oh, man. Your company, chocolate chip cookies, a walk on the beach—you're tearing at my heart. But, we're *so* close. I need to nail this tonight. If I'm right, I'll be home for several days beginning tomorrow—lots of walking, time together, and loads of chocolate chip cookies."

"I love you, Lou. Give me a call when you're on your way."

"I love you, too. And yes, I'll call with an ETA."

Lou hung up and looked at Jack, "Well if I do die tonight, at least my last words to Carol were that I loved her."

"Nothing is going to happen to you, Lou," Jack said confidently.

"We never know, Jack. We just never know. Got to be thankful for every minute."

Lou and Jack returned to their discussion. "It would be great if there was a man that had a rock on a finger of his left hand in the car with Christy. "

"Yeah, that would be incriminating."

"Hey, got to hand it to the youth in this community," Jack said.

"Yes, Sara and Tim were quite helpful. They have good values. I just hope Sara isn't scarred by this experience."

✿

Late that afternoon, a man entered the police station and approached the reception window. The female officer acting as receptionist slid the window to one side and asked, "How can I help you?"

"Is Mr. Searing here?"

"Yes, I believe so. Do you need to see him?"

"No. I was just wondering if he was here is all. Thanks." The man turned and left the station. Chief Bixler had forgotten to tell the staff to keep Lou's presence to themselves.

The receptionist came into the conference room, got Lou's attention and said, "A man was just in here looking for you. I said you were here, but he said he didn't need to see you, he only wondered if you were here."

Lou said nothing. He just shook his head side-to-side and took a deep breath. "From now on, don't let *anyone* know I'm here, OK?"

"Yes, sir."

"Do you have a security camera in the reception area?"

"Yes, we do."

"I want to see who came looking for me. How can I review the tape?"

"We'll set that up for you. It will show on that television monitor over there," the officer said pointing to the corner of the room.

"You see, Jack?" Lou flustered, turning away from the door. "All it takes is one small slip-up like that to destroy a plan, and maybe a life. I'm not scared, Jack, but sometimes I wish I didn't know what I know."

Fifteen minutes later an officer turned on the television monitor and played the tape from the man's entering the station.

"This is the guy you're asking about," the officer said.

Lou and Jack looked intently at the monitor.

"He doesn't look like anyone I know," Jack said.

"I'm in the dark as well." Lou asked the officer in the reception area to join them for another viewing. She appeared shortly.

"You're trained to study body language," Lou said. "Tell us about this man—did he seem nervous? Did his voice sound strange?"

"No. He seemed quite normal," the officer replied. "Actually, I think Chief Bixler knows him."

"Is she in the station now?" Lou asked.

"No, she went over to the courthouse, but I expect her any minute." Ten seconds later, she said, "I hear her now. Chief!" She called. "Please come in here."

Chief Bixler entered the room. "Do you know this man?" Lou asked as the officer replayed the tape.

"Sure. That's Zeb Horvath, owner of the men's clothing store."

"He came in here, asked if I was here, and when told I was, said he didn't need to see me," Lou explained. "Very strange."

"Yes, but I imagine he wanted to get an idea of what you looked like. He's going to dress the dummy for us to take to the winery. You know, height, style of clothes, that sort of thing."

"But, he didn't see me. He just asked if I were here and then left."

"I can't explain that, but it's nothing to do with the threat on your life. He's a good guy. He probably saw my parking enforcement officer in the lot and high-tailed it back to his car. He'll probably be back soon, but if he doesn't come back, I'll call for an explanation."

"I'd appreciate it," Lou said.

⚜

Lou and Jack were getting bored being confined to the police station, but that was the plan, and with any luck, the case would be solved by sundown.

Jack asked Lou, "When you served your search warrant, did you find an audit report?"

"No. Now that the office was destroyed, we'll never see that or any report."

"Don't bet on it, Lou. I saw the cover of the audit on an earlier visit to the winery and wrote down the phone number of the CPA firm that handled it. The name on it was Tom Robinson. I'll call him unless you object."

"Fine with me. What do you expect to learn?" Lou asked.

"Nothing. But, it was something on Christy's desk. It can't hurt to talk to the auditor."

Jack found a phone book and located the firm, Robinson and Brooks. Using his cell phone he called and was surprised to have the phone answered by Mr. Robinson.

Jack explained who he was, and the reason for his call.

"Actually, I'm glad you called. I thought of calling Stacy, but just didn't."

"What's on your mind?"

"Well, we recently conducted that audit of the Northernmost Winery, and I discovered some major discrepancies. I wondered if the problem at the winery had some bearing on the murder."

"Please tell me what you discovered."

"With Tom being dead, I don't imagine he would object. I couldn't account for tens of thousands of dollars. I told Tom about the problem a couple of days before he was murdered."

"How did he react?" Jack asked.

"He was livid. I remember hoping he had taken his blood pressure medicine because he was so upset I thought blood vessels would pop."

"Did he have an explanation for the missing money?"

"No. He did say he would talk with Christy."

"Why Christy?" Jack asked. "Seems like he would talk to the financial director."

"I agree. But, he definitely mentioned Christy."

"Did he ever use the word 'embezzle'?"

"No. I didn't get the impression he thought Christy stole the money. I think he simply wanted to discuss the problem with his manager."

"Thank you for talking with me. I'll tell Lou about your findings. He may want to speak with you."

"Fine. I want to help, so if Lou has questions, by all means, have him call."

"Thank you very much, Mr. Robinson."

Chief Bixler appeared. "I called Zeb at the clothing store. He left because he realized your photo is on the back of your books. And your description appears early in each book, so he really didn't need to bother you. He figured you were busy working the case, and he didn't want to interrupt. Since the dummy will be seen only from the back, he didn't need to see *you*. But he would like to meet you someday, if possible."

"Okay, I feel better now," Lou said, relieved.

"Also, here is an update. Security on the Badger has confirmed that Christy is on board, and a man is with her—a man sporting quite a rock on his left hand. Finally, the crossing is on time. State Police will trail Christy and the man when they drive away from the dock, and they'll give us updates as they approach Traverse City."

"Thanks for the update, Chief."

⁂

Sara and Mrs. Laskey were having a vacation of sorts in Northport. Mother-daughter time seemed to be just what the doctor ordered. They talked about everything under the sun. Mrs. Laskey told Sara about her childhood growing up in Petoskey, they listened to music, and Mrs. Laskey sampled some of Sara's favorite rock stars' music. The two even put together a complicated jigsaw puzzle, the first activity they had done together since making sugar cookies when Sara was five.

"I sure hope Mr. Searing and Mr. Kelly either have solved the case or are close to solving it," Sara said.

"We've seen nothing in the newspaper about it. I imagine when it's finished we'll go home," Mrs. Laskey said.

"Actually, I hope we can spend the entire week here," Sara said. "I'm having a wonderful time with you." The two hugged while standing on the porch looking out at the calm, blue waters of Grand Traverse Bay.

⁂

Lou was still holed up at the police station when Carol called again. "Hello. Those chocolate chip cookies still for sale?" Lou asked.

"Lou, are you okay?" Carol asked, sounding quite distressed.

"Sure am."

"I've had a premonition. You know, like I had when your uncle Howard died, and when Slater Wristen's foot was cut off by a lawn mower."

"What's the premonition?" Lou asked.

"It's *you,* Lou. I sense danger. I'm *scared,* Lou."

"Listen, everything is fine. It must be your imagination. I'm in the Traverse City police station with Jack. How much safer can I be?"

"I'm glad *you're* confident. My premonitions are rare, but they have come true. I think I'm going to be sick, Lou. I love you." The phone went dead.

Lou called their son, Scott, in Grand Rapids. "I need your help, son."

"Sure, what do you need?"

"I need you and Patti to go stay with Nana. She's had a premonition that something terrible is going to happen to me."

"Oh, boy," Scott said. He had heard of previous premonitions that became reality.

"Nana is really scared, sick to her stomach. I'm going to call our doctor next, but I need you and Patti to be with her."

"We'll head out the door right now. We should be there in about 40 minutes."

"Thanks, son."

"Not a problem. Are you in trouble, Father? Could her premonition be on target?"

"Yes, but I'm being protected. I'll keep you informed, and you can decide what to tell Nana. We hope to capture the killer within a few hours. After that, I'll call to let you know I'm safe."

"Okay. I love you."

"Love you too, son. Take care of Nana, please."

Lou called their family doctor and explained the stress that Carol was experiencing. The on-call physician promised someone would attend to Carol as soon as possible. Lou then called Marie, their next-door neighbor. He explained that Scott and Patti would be arriving in about a half-hour, but in the meantime would she stay with Carol till they arrived? Marie said, of course she would.

⁂

Chief Bixler came back into the conference room. "Officers are at the winery as we speak, setting up the model in the tasting room. Actually, I've seen the mannequin, and the thing looks like your twin brother, Lou."

"I guess that's reassuring," Lou replied.

"And, Christy and a man got off the Badger, entered a vehicle, and have just turned north on 31 heading for Manistee. Their ETA in Traverse City is 8:15."

"Does the man with Christy have a large ring on his left hand?" Lou asked.

"Yes. A picture of the two of them should arrive by fax soon. We'll see if he's recognizable."

As Chief Bixler finished her comment, an officer entered and set the photo of Christy and the man on the table. Six eyes immediately took the image into their consciousness.

"Is this anybody we know?" Chief Bixler asked.

"I've never seen him," Lou said.

"I don't recognize him," Chief Bixler admitted.

"I think he is Joanne's Tuttle's husband, Steve," Jack said. "I saw a guy in Carl's Tire Store. I assumed he was Carl, but this is Joanne's husband. I'm sure of it."

"Very good eyes, Jack," Lou said.

"I'm not surprised," Jack replied. "I thought when I saw him that he might be involved."

"Something he said?" Lou asked.

"No, just a gut feeling I get once in a while."

Lou called Carol to see how she was doing. Marie answered the phone and said Carol was talking to the doctor, who had just arrived, and that she seemed to have calmed down a bit. "Please tell her that I'm fine and that Scott and Patti will arrive in about twenty minutes."

"OK, Lou. She seemed pleased to see me at the door but she immediately began sobbing and saying that something terrible might happen to you."

"Please try to reassure her that I'm fine and *will be* fine."

"I will, Lou. See you when you get home."

"Thanks, Marie."

᪥⚘᪥

The car carrying Christy and Joanne's husband continued toward Traverse City. After passing Interlochen and Grawn, it turned north. As they got closer to town, the two pulled into a McDonald's staying in the drive-up lane. After getting their order, they pulled into a parking space and shut off the engine.

About fifteen minutes later a vehicle pulled in beside them. A woman got out and got into the car with Christy.

"I didn't think you'd ever get here," Christy snapped.

"Sorry, traffic was slow for some reason. I would have left earlier, but my boss demands the big hand strike five before I move."

"Stone called. Lou is working at the winery this evening, in the tasting room going over paperwork. I guess they saved a lot of records and computers before the bomb went off."

"Is the plan still to kill him?" Joanne asked.

"It's either him or us. He's an investigator who always solves the crime. Either we take him out, or we'll be behind bars for a long time."

As the three pulled away, Joanne asked. "So, bring me up to speed here. We're going to drive to the winery, find Lou, and shoot him, right?"

"It is not quite that simple. We'll pick up Stone first. When we get to the winery, we'll park on the side of the road and walk back. Stone will go to the tasting room and talk with

Lou. Steve will position himself so that he can get the cross-hairs on the middle of Lou's back. Once Stone is safely out of the way, Steve fires. We hustle back to the car hoping Lou won't be discovered until tomorrow."

"Sounds like you've got everything covered," Joanne said, impressed with the detailed plan.

"I think so," Christy said. "If anything interrupts the plan, we simply pull back and figure another way to put him away."

"I saw in the paper that you weren't very successful at tossing that girl into the Straits," Joanne said.

"No. She got loose and found the tire iron. When we opened the trunk to get her out, she went wild, kicking and screaming and flailing. She took off running and eventually ran into a state cop. They didn't catch us, though. We got into the U.P. and headed west."

⚘

Lou and Jack remained in the Traverse City police station, staying up-to-date with Christy's, Joanne's and Steve's movements. At the winery, officers had parked Lou's car in a small lot outside the tasting room. The mannequin was upright and looked like Lou from the back. A light was on so Steve would have good lighting for shooting.

Christy had told Stone Elliott to monitor Lou and Jack's movements. But, since he had jumped ship to help the law, Stone was free to live his day as planned. He was to meet the three at Bryant Park off M-37 at the base of Old Mission Peninsula. Christy would call Stone when they were about a half-hour away. That would give him time to drive to the park, bringing a rifle and ammunition.

Christy called Stone to report a change in plans. Joanne had heard that the girl who saw the killer get into the motor home was staying with her mother in Northport. As they drove into downtown Traverse City, Christy suggested they alter their course.

"Maybe killing Searing is not the best alternative. If we keep with our plan, I'm afraid we'd be discovered, sooner, if not later."

"I've been thinking the same thing," Joanne added.

"On the other hand, if we try again to take out the girl, and can do it cleanly, we're back to that perfect crime; no witnesses, no weapon, no clear motive, and as far as we know, no suspects," Christy reasoned. "If we take down Searing, we're starting over, and we may not be as lucky the second time around."

"Faulty reasoning," Joanne said. "If we take out the girl, we're starting over, and we definitely would not be as lucky as the first time."

"Here's something else to consider," Steve said, breaking into the conversation. "If the girl is missed, there will be a lot of police checkpoints because the peninsula would be our only escape route—south. We can't go north, east, or west. We're surrounded by water."

"That settles it—forget the girl!" Christy announced. "We stay with our plan to take out Searing. We know where he is, he's isolated, and working alone. Nobody will see us."

"At least, we hope not," Joanne added.

Christy called Stone to confirm the pick-up. The sun was beginning to set when the car with four occupants pulled up to the entrance of the Northernmost Winery. They parked on the shoulder of the road about 500 feet beyond the entrance.

"Okay, let's go over it again," Christy said. "We walk back to the winery. Stone goes into the tasting room to talk to Searing. When he leaves Searing, we'll have a caged animal ready for execution. He mustn't see us; if by some freakish chance, he lives, we don't want him to remember us. Okay, Steve, you have the rifle and it's loaded, right?" Christy asked.

"I'm all set," Steve responded.

"Okay, let's go."

✿❀❈

When Scott and Patti arrived at the Searing home, they found Carol sedated, for the doctor had decided a calming drug was indicated. Carol told Scott about her premonition, concluding with, "I fear your father will not come home alive. My premonitions are rare, but they're often a glimpse of reality. I'm so thankful you're here."

"We're glad to help," Scott said, giving Carol a hug. "Father called me, and he sounded great. I got no indication he's looking at death. He's close to wrapping up the case, and I suppose that can be threatening, but he'll be just fine. Of that I'm certain."

Patti cleaned up the kitchen before giving Scott a break from sitting with Carol in the den. Samm, the Searing's golden retriever, was doing her job too, sitting calmly at Carol's feet, giving reassurance that all would be well.

The report from the winery was that the sting was in place. Once a shot was fired, the police would intervene and make the arrests, and the drama would be over. Chief Bixler walked over to Lou, "Want to be part of the surprise?"

"How do you mean?"

"We could drive out to the winery, and while my officers move the criminals to our van you could get out and look them right in the eye. They'll think you're dead in the tasting room. Can you imagine the looks on their faces when they see you standing in the driveway?"

"That might be satisfying, but playing games is not my style. I'd rather stay here until we get word that the four of them—well actually three—are in custody. Once I hear that, and my car is back here, I'm heading home. My wife had a premonition that something terrible was going to happen to me, and I need to assure her that I'm safe."

"I understand. Actually, I can't believe I suggested we drive out there. That's not my MO. The image just popped into my head, and I expressed it rather than dismissing it. Sorry."

⁕❀⁕

At the winery, the four were about to execute their plan. Stone rapped on the door of the tasting room before he entered. He walked up to the mannequin, put his hand on its shoulder, and pretended to talk to Lou. Knowing he was being watched from outside, he made sure he didn't knock over the dummy or dislodge any of the clothes. After a minute of animated talking to the mannequin, Stone turned and walked out the door. Once Stone was out of the way, Steve walked to the door, quietly opened it, and fired three shots into the mannequin. He slammed the door and ran without seeing that he had simply toppled a mannequin in a cheap suit.

The four exchanged high-fives, then turned to walk back to the road, only to encounter a dozen officers with guns drawn. The four were ordered to the ground, where they were hand-cuffed and searched for weapons.

Detective Morrison called Chief Bixler. "One of the men fired three rounds into the dummy; he didn't realize his 'victim' was not human. All four are in custody, searched and handcuffed. We'll load them into the van and bring them in for processing."

"Excellent job, Morrison. Jack and Lou will be relieved, to say the least."

As predicted, Lou and Jack both heaved a sigh of relief. As soon as Lou's car was back at the police station, they thanked Chief Bixler for her work in apprehending the four.

"We're heading south now," Lou said. "I'll be back soon to wrap this up for you."

"It's been a long day for you two," Chief Bixler replied. "Drive safely. And, please thank your families for putting up with your staying here and risking your lives."

"Will do." Lou and Jack walked to their cars and began the three-hour trip to Muskegon and Grand Haven, respectively.

✿❀✿

The criminals did not yet know that Stone had turned against them. They couldn't figure out how their plan had been discovered, since they had only talked among themselves.

The four were brought to the county jail and processed. They would be kept overnight and arraigned in the morning. Christy called a lawyer, one of the best in the area, Walter Hagen, named like the golfer. He had represented the winery several times, but this was the first time he would represent a winery employee.

Walter came to the jail even though it was nearly eleven at night. Before he talked with his four clients, he sought out Detective Morrison, to determine the charges that Christy and the others faced.

"They're charged with shooting a *mannequin?*" attorney Hagen nearly shouted, shocked by the accusation. "Tell me again! I don't believe what I'm hearing!"

"Yes, it was a mannequin, but the shooter fully believed that it was Lou Searing. So, in a sense, Lou Searing was a 'victim'."

Hagan paced the floor. "You folks never cease to amaze me. These stories just get weirder and weirder. Let me hear it one more time." He suddenly stopped dead and turned to Morrison, "No, *I'll* tell *you* what happened, and you tell me whether I'm right. Four people drove out to the winery, the place where they work and have a right to be on the property."

"Two of them work there, yes."

"Whatever. One of them goes into the tasting room and talks to a mannequin. So far, am I right?"

"Yes."

"He finishes talking to the mannequin and leaves the tasting room. Presently, a man fires a rifle at the mannequin, and it falls. Right?"

"Yes."

"And you then arrest these people for *murder?*"

"Of course."

"So, let's say that you're on patrol when you pass a farm. You see a kid shooting a bow and arrow into one of those wooden deer. Do you pull over and arrest the kid for murder?"

"Don't be ridiculous, Mr. Hagen."

"Exactly my point," Walter replied in a loud voice. "I assure you that no judge in his right mind will hold a citizen for shooting at a mannequin. Preposterous, Detective Morrison, simply preposterous. I'll have these people out of jail tonight. Now, charges for damaging a mannequin, or replacing damaged property in the tasting room, or firing a rifle on private property, that's a different story. But murder? Not a prayer, Detective. Excuse me. I'm going to talk with Chief Bixler and get my clients out of here."

The Chief had contacted the county prosecuting attorney and explained the sting operation, hoping Theodore "Ted" Walsh would be comfortable moving forward with the charges and a trial.

"Something about this doesn't sound right," the prosecutor mused upon hearing the story. "Did you run this plan by anyone on my staff before executing it?"

"No, I didn't feel the need. Police agencies often use sting operations to trick criminals into implicating themselves. In our sting, the suspects clearly believed Lou Searing was standing in the tasting room with his back to the door. In the mind of the shooter, the target was Lou Searing. We're not talking about target practice—we're talking about attempted murder!"

"I've got to look into this, Chief. This will either embarrass you or make you a hero. We'll keep the four overnight, so my staff and I have some time to look up case law."

Chief Bixler patiently listened to Attorney Hagen's arguments, but insisted that the four would not be brought before a judge until the morning. The police would let the legal system play out. But, she added, "Walter, we've been friends for a long time. Nobody respects you more than I do, so I'm going to let you in on something. Your client, Christy, is also a suspect in the kidnapping of a thirteen-year-old girl, driving her to the Mackinac Bridge in the trunk, bound hand and foot, fully intending to throw her into the Straits. The girl broke free, fought her captors off, and ran against traffic until she encountered a state trooper. Your client is in very deep. And, I'll tell you this: if I lose tomorrow on some technicality, Christy will immediately be charged with the kidnapping of a minor with intent to murder. And, there are even bigger fish to fry. I can't prove it yet, but it's possible your client eventually will be charged with the murder of Tom NcNutt. So, clear your calendar, Walt, because you've a lot of work ahead."

Walter then met with his clients to hear their side of the story.

Chief Bixler called Lou to brief him on the activities of the last hour.

"Everything okay with you, Lou? If you get drowsy, be sure and pull off for a nap."

"I'm doing well. I found an FM station with good music. And, I called and talked with Carol. She's calmer, thankful I'm out of Traverse City."

"I'll call again later if I have anything to tell you."

"That's fine. I can see some pretty strong lightning over Lake Michigan. Are heavy storms forecast for tonight?"

"I don't know. My head has been totally in this case. I can check weather reports for you."

"That's okay, I'll monitor the weather on the radio. Talk to you soon. Thanks for the update."

"You're welcome, Lou."

꧁❀꧂

Lou called his son to report his progress. "I'm getting there Scott, but it looks like powerful storms to the west."

"You're right," Scott replied. "According to the television weatherman, a line of storms will come ashore with a vengeance."

"I hope I get home before they hit."

"Listen, Father. Just stay in a motel till this blows over. What's a hundred bucks for a room, compared to dangerous road conditions? Nana is already stressed out enough, and knowing you're safe in a motel would do wonders for her. In fact, I can't think of a better gift for her than a phone call from a motel room in Manistee or Ludington or wherever."

"You're right, son. I'll do it."

"Even I'm relieved. Thanks," Scott took a deep breath. "We'll wait for your call." Motels with vacancy signs seemed not to exist. But a bed and breakfast in Ludington had one room left, so Lou claimed it and wrote his name in the register book.

"You were wise to get inside, Mr. Searing," the innkeeper said. "Nobody in his right mind will be outside for the next couple of hours."

"That's what my son said. I'll be safe here."

"We're happy to have you. Here's the key—on your right at the top of the stairs. A full breakfast begins at seven-thirty tomorrow morning—unless we're floating out to sea by then." Both chuckled.

Although it was after midnight, Lou called Carol, "I'm at a bed and breakfast in Ludington. Scott convinced me to get out of the storms."

"I'm so thankful, Lou. Scott and Patti have been wonderful. They're staying overnight with me. Grandson Ben has everything under control at their house."

"Good. Now, *you* get some sleep. No more worry. I'll be home late tomorrow morning."

"I love you, Lou."

"I love you like a rock, Sweetzie."

Lou next called Jack to see where he was. Jack answered on the first ring. "Hi, Lou. Have you found a port? Are you riding out this storm?"

"I'm at a B and B in Ludington. Where are you?"

"Further down the coast than you—I think I can make it home. From weather reports, it seems the heart of the storm will hit near you."

"Be careful, my friend."

"Likewise, Lou."

Jack made it home ahead of the storm, and Elaine was relieved to see him pull into the driveway.

CHAPTER NINE

Day 6 • July 11

Lou slept through the storm. With his hearing loss he heard nothing, although there was plenty to hear. The storm was deafening enough, but sirens of emergency vehicles sounded throughout the night.

Lou enjoyed the breakfast which was as good as the meal at the Wellington Inn. French toast, sausage, a sweet roll, and a helping of scrambled eggs, along with coffee and orange juice provided a delicious start to the day.

The front had gone through and the threat of another storm was nil, but there was plenty to clean up. Lou was thankful this wasn't a snowstorm because he would have been snowed in and gone nowhere but back to bed. Lou took his time packing and preparing to leave. As he paid his bill, he realized that every dollar was well-spent.

In the B & B parking lot, Lou found once again that he had been lucky. A heavy branch had snapped from a large oak bordering the lot, but the limb had missed Lou's car. If he were a cat, he would have used up three of his nine lives in one night. He liked to think he had a half-dozen lives left.

Lou noted many signs of the storm as he drove out of town. Traffic lights were out, and intersections were flooded. He also saw the aftermath of several automobile accidents. The landscape was eerie. While Lou had never seen a tornado, the damage in Ludington must have been like a tornado's aftermath.

Lou encountered no problems once he got onto the four-lane. Traffic was light for most people had remained in their homes inspecting damage or staying off roads so emergency vehicles could move easily. Lou pressed on to Muskegon, and then to Grand Haven. He pulled into his driveway and into Carol's arms about ten-thirty. Samm joined in the greeting with happy barks and wags of her tail.

❀

Stone told Christy, Joanne, and Steve that he was sorry, but he decided he couldn't be part of Lou Searing's murder, or any murder for that matter. The trio were angry with him for having destroyed their plans and finding themselves behind bars, but they all learned a lesson in trust.

The three suspects were brought before Judge Ponstein at eleven in the morning, when they heard charges against them. Walter Hagen spoke forcefully about his clients being arrested without cause. "Your honor, in this country, county, or city, you cannot be charged with attempted murder for shooting a mannequin!"

The county prosecutor disagreed, citing legal precedents for such action. "Your honor, in numerous cases suspects have been lured into a trap to catch them in the act of violence. In addition, the action by the Traverse City Police was taken to save the life of an investigator who has earned great respect in our community. Not to have acted could have led to another murder."

The judge listened to both sides of the argument, then asked the defendants how they pled. All three said, "Not guilty, your Honor." The judge ordered the case to trial. Because Lou Searing's life had been threatened, the judge ruled that the three were remanded to the county jail.

Chief Bixler called Lou to report what had happened in the county courthouse. "I appreciate your call, Chief. Jack and I are going to stay put for at least a day, so please give us any updates, and I'll let you know if we uncover anything of interest. Oh, by the way, I want to talk to the young man who saw the ring worn by the man coming out of the queen's float."

"Certainly. I'll ask Rod to give you a call."

"Thank you, Chief."

"Was Carol glad to see you home safely?"

"That's an understatement, if ever there was one. Yes, Carol, Samm, and I are thankful to be together, safe and sound."

✿❀✿

For the first time in nearly a week, the energy around the McNutt murder case eased. Lou relaxed now that Christy, Joanne, and Steve were behind bars. But the question lingered: who came out of the queen's float wearing the ring? Lou wouldn't feel he had completely solved the case without identifying that man. Or perhaps, that *woman*.

Jack called in the early afternoon. "Got a minute, Lou?"

"Always, for you. Go ahead."

"I can't wrap my mind around the boat on Sanford Lake and the blind woman's recollection of someone dropping a bag into the lake. So, I got a list of cabin-owners from the County Register of Deeds, and I compared the owners with the cabin's locations. A couple of names showed up that I think you'll find interesting."

"Rather than playing twenty questions, why don't you just tell me?"

"Okay, take my fun out of it, see if I care," Jack said with a chuckle. "One name is Gerald Johnson, with a deed signed by him and a 'Crystal,' which could be 'Christy.' Their cabin is several lots to the left of the Albers' cabin. So the boat, if theirs, would come into view from the left if it were rowed straight out into the lake."

"The second owner?" Lou asked.

"Well, this name has come up in the investigation, but he was dismissed as a suspect. The deed belongs to Eric and Gloria Williams."

"Who?"

"The driver of the Grand Marshal vehicle. You know, the one who wound up in second place in the voting for the Grand Marshal."

"Interesting. Good work, Jack."

"Their cabin is two doors down from the Johnson cabin, so I assume a rowboat taken from the Williams cottage would go to the same general area in the middle of the lake."

"One of the things I admire about Detective Morrison is his ability to always second-guess a comment," Lou remarked. "Having a cabin on Lake Sanford does not a murderer make. Ownership of a cabin in and of itself should not raise a suspicion of murder."

"I realize that. All I'm saying is that these two names are associated with cabins on Sanford Lake where a bag was dropped into the water, the day of, or following, McNutt's murder. Johnson or Williams may have nothing to do with the murder, but we need this information in our files."

"Absolutely, Jack. Again, excellent work!"

❦❀❦

Lou got Tim Jacobs' phone number. He called and asked to speak with Mr. or Mrs. Jacobs. Mrs. Jacobs came on the line.

"Mrs. Jacobs, this is Lou Searing calling. I'm assisting the Traverse City police in investigating the murder of Thomas McNutt."

"Yes, so I've heard."

"I'd like to talk to Tim about what he saw the morning of the parade, but first, I'd like your permission to do so. Also, I would like you to stay on the phone so you can hear what I ask and what your son says. If you feel your attorney should participate, we can set up a conference call."

"I'm agreeable, but let me call our attorney and get her reading on it."

"Please call me back when decisions are made."

The family attorney thought it fine for Tim to talk with Lou, and she didn't need to listen in. She agreed with Lou, however, that Mrs. Jacobs should be on the line. If the boy was uncomfortable answering a question, he didn't need to answer.

Mrs. Jacobs called Lou back and explained what her attorney had said. Tim was beside her and ready to talk.

"First of all," Lou said, "I want to commend you for coming forward and reporting what you saw the morning of the Cherry Festival Parade. You're a brave fellow."

"Thank you."

"I have a couple of questions for you regarding that incident. Okay?"

"Sure."

"How certain are you that the person wearing the ring you described had been inside the queen's float?"

"One hundred percent."

"You didn't see him with a gun, did you? I mean, you would have told the police if you'd seen one."

"Yes, I would have told them, for sure!"

"Could the man with the ring have been Mr. Williams going from inside the queen's float to the driver's seat of the Grand Marshal vehicle in the confusion."

"I don't think the man was Mr. Williams."

"You said 'I don't think…' Are you sure the man was *not* Mr. Williams?"

"Yes, I'm sure. The man was *not* Mr. Williams."

"And you can say this because you could pick him out of a crowd."

"Yes, I know him. His son, Junior Williams, was a coach on the football team."

"That brings up an interesting point. Could the man coming out of the float have been his son, Junior?"

"No, the man with the ring was not Coach Williams. I'm *certain* of that."

"Did you see the man with the ring go inside the float, or did you only see him come out?"

"Come out."

"So you wouldn't know how long he was inside the float?"

"No, I wouldn't."

"Thank you, Tim. Again, you are a fine representative of Traverse City youth."

"Thank you, Mr. Searing."

※❀※

It turned out to be a beautiful day along the eastern shore of Lake Michigan. Scott and Patti returned to see how Nana was doing, and so that their sons could go for a swim in the Lake. Lou once again thanked Scott for his advice to find a bed for the night.

While the younger Searings were swimming, Jack Kelly appeared at the door. Lou opened the door and greeted Jack. Jack seeing a family gathering said, "Oh, I didn't realize your family was visiting. I'll come back another time."

"No, come on in, you're practically family. In fact, if you've come to talk about the case, Nick would probably like to listen in. He's expressed some interest in writing, or perhaps pursuing a career in forensic science. But I think the real reason you came over was for Carol's chocolate chip cookies. Am I right?"

"To be honest, that did come to mind."

"Come on in and make yourself at home."

Lou got Jack a Diet Pepsi and called out the back door, "Hey, Nick! Come here for a minute, OK?"

Thirteen year-old Nick grabbed a towel and ran up to the house, not because he was in a hurry, but because the sand was so hot under his feet. He washed his feet off at the outside faucet, dried them, and went inside. "You wanted me, Grandpa?"

"Nick, you remember Mr. Kelly, don't you?"

"Sure. Hi, Mr. Kelly."

"Great day for the beach, huh, Nick?" Jack asked.

"Sure is."

"Mr. Kelly and I are going to talk about a case we're working on in Traverse City. With your recent interests in writing and forensic science, I thought you might like to listen in, maybe ask a reporter's question or two."

"Okay. Thanks!"

"If you'd rather be in the lake, we understand."

"No, this is great! Thanks for inviting me to listen."

Lou took a few minutes to state the basic facts about the case and the work to date. "We decided to stay at home instead of Traverse City. It gives us a chance to unwind and put our heads together for some serious analysis. With my introduction out of the way, Jack is going to say what's on his mind."

"First, why would the killer make the decisions he or she made to carry out this crime? I mean, look at the stupidity. The killer comes into town in a motor home, which she or he stole some twenty miles away. Why this huge vehicle? Then she/he kills the victim in broad daylight with thousands of people around. Now we find that the killer supposedly was wearing a large jeweled ring on his left hand, an obvious identifier. Either we have the most naïve criminal ever, or there was a method to his—or her—madness."

"Maybe the ring was to throw off the police," Nick replied, getting right into the analysis. "Maybe the killer did that to set up someone else in Traverse City who owns a ring like that. It would take attention off him and put it on someone people know who wears that kind of ring."

Jack said, "Good thinking, Nick."

Lou resumed. "I'm trying to envision what happened the day of the murder. By that I mean the number of people involved and the logistics of…"

"Grandpa, what does that word mean?" Nick asked.

"Logistics?"

"Yeah."

"Logistics means strategic movement of people and supplies. It is a military term."

"Thanks." Nick was satisfied.

Lou continued. "Two people take separate cars to the county park. They leave one car in the park and then both go to the gas station to look for a vehicle to steal. Once the vehicle is stolen, the second vehicle leaves for wherever they will meet after the crime. If I'm right, only one killer takes the vehicle to Traverse City, commits the crime, and then dumps the motor home at the county park. Then the killer drives the car left for him/her in the park to wherever the second person has gone for safe hiding."

"That's how I see it," Jack replied.

"As for your questions about the place for the murder, I don't have answers. It leaves me in a quandary as well."

"Grandpa, what does *that* word mean?"

"Quandary means a state of confusion or uncertainty."

"Thanks."

"The motive for the death is still unclear. Do you agree?" Jack asked.

"If the people who plotted my death are behind McNutt's murder, one motive could be McNutt not participating in an annulment from his marriage to Joanne. A motive for Christy is probably McNutt about to confront her with embezzling money."

The discussion was interrupted by the phone in the kitchen. "I'll get it," Lou shouted. The caller was Mrs. Jacobs. "Tim just mentioned something to me that I thought you should know. When he was student of the month last January, he was invited to the Rotary Club to accept the award. As part of the meeting, the club presented a 'Super Bowl Ring of Service' to the member who had provided outstanding community service during the past year. It's a nice ring, but it's mostly glass. Tim said it was a serious award, but he didn't think the ring was very valuable."

"This is helpful, Mrs. Jacobs. Please thank Tim for passing this on."

Lou returned to Jack and Nick, carrying several chocolate chip cookies, and reported what he had learned.

"Looks like the killer may be a member of Rotary, and a distinguished member at that," Nick replied, taking the cookie with the most chocolate chips.

"If it's the same ring, my guess is what Nick said earlier— a ploy to put official attention on a Rotary Club member."

"McNutt's ex-wife, Joanne, and Christy both would have known about this ring, because Thomas McNutt must have received the award—perhaps more than once," Lou explained. "If he had it during his marriage to Joanne, or if he kept it on his desk or displayed it somewhere in his office, Christy would know about it."

Jack added, "Eric Williams probably got one too, and he was the driver of the Grand Marshal vehicle. Williams is showing up more and more in this drama. He was close to McNutt prior to the parade start. He has a cabin on Sanford Lake, where evidence may have been hidden. He came in second to McNutt in the contest for Grand Marshal."

"That wouldn't make someone kill, would it?" Nick asked.

"Nick, you'd be surprised at the reasons people have for killing. What you or I would consider reasonable, others see differently."

"I don't think there is *any* reason to kill another," Nick said.

"That's great," Jack replied. "You hold on to that, Nick, and it will serve you well."

"We had better wind this up," Lou said, gathering his notes. "The cookies are gone, Nick has lost valuable swim time in Lake Michigan, and I need to start a fire for hotdogs and hamburgers this evening. Can you stay for dinner, Jack?"

"Thanks, but no. I told Elaine I'd be home around this time, so I need to leave."

"Before you go, I want to talk about the obvious killer," Lou stated. "I throw Eric Williams into the ring."

"I'll see your 'Eric Williams,' and play my 'Christy Johnson' card," Jack replied.

"I'll raise you both with the 'Joanne' card," Nick ended the betting.

"Anyone else?" Lou asked.

"Christy's husband," Jack added.

"I agree," Lou replied.

"There are a number of minor possibilities, but I don't think they rank very high," Jack said.

"Like who?" Lou asked.

"Like, the brew master and the two employees that were fired. Like, McNutt's current wife. Like Corky, who is incensed at losing a lot of customers in this area," Jack explained.

Lou continued, "Like an angry ocean sailor who has an axe to grind with McNutt over something in the sailing world. Like Father Pat who…"

"Father Pat?" Nick asked astonished.

"Oh, I just threw him on the pile to see how you would react."

"You had me wondering there for a minute," Nick said, smiling.

"When we go back to Traverse City, we'll show photos of our suspects to Tim Jacobs and see how he reacts," Lou stated.

"And, we will show the same photos to Sara Laskey," Jack added.

Jack had one more possible motive. "We thought it odd that the winery was using out-of-state grapes. I thought that practice might enter into this case, but I guess we can rule it out."

"Yes, I think we can. Okay, meeting over," Lou declared. "Thanks for coming down from Muskegon, Jack. Thanks for giving us some time out of the water, Nick."

It was a marvelous evening for the Searings' picnic on the beach. They sang songs, enjoyed s'mores as the sun started to slide into Wisconsin, threw footballs and Frisbees, and couples walked hand in hand. Samm seemed to enjoy having so many people around. When the evening on the beach was coming to an end, they all joined hands and Lou led a prayer of thanks for family, for fun times, and for all blessings. After the prayer, the younger Searings left for Grand Rapids, and Lou and Carol cleaned up. They stood on the back porch, watching a three-quarter moon shine over the lake. They held hands, and then gave each other a prolonged hug.

"I'm so thankful you are all right, Lou."

"Yes, and I love you for being so concerned and kind."

"We're pretty lucky people, Lou. We are richly blessed."

"Indeed."

CHAPTER TEN

Day 7 • July 12

On this the second full day of rest for Lou and Jack, Lou talked with Detective Morrison asking that a set of photos be prepared to show to Sara and Tim. Detective Morrison would head to Northport for Sara's reaction, then return to Traverse City and show the same set to Tim.

"I'll call you with whatever I learn," Detective Morrison promised.

"I'd like to be with you, but it is a long way to drive for what I imagine will happen."

"And that would be?"

"I expect Sara will identify Christy as the one who abducted her at the funeral home. I expect Tim to say that it was Christy and *not* her husband who came out from inside the front of the queen's float wearing the huge ring."

"That's my prediction as well."

"Do you have any idea what's behind the murder of Tom McNutt?"

"Do you mean you want my 'Colonel Mustard did it in the kitchen with a rope' statement?" Lou said.

"Let me hear it."

"Christy did it with a .38 caliber pistol with a silencer from inside the queen's float. Joanne Tuttle teamed with the Johnsons because, if Tom were dead, she could marry within the church. Christy wanted Tom dead, because she discovered that Tom was going to confront her about embezzling company money to support her gambling."

"Those are my thoughts to the letter," Rod Morrison replied. "Great minds think alike."

Lou continued. "Christy fully believed that Sara Laskey knew more than she did. In reality, Sara never saw the face of the woman and wouldn't have recognized her if she came to the door. Christy's imagination just ran wild, and she felt she had to kill Sara in order to protect her perfect crime."

In mid-afternoon Lou got the call he had been expecting. Detective Morrison reported what the teens' reactions had been to the photos. As predicted, Sara identified Christy and Joanne's husband, Steve, as her abductors. Their pictures were the only photos she could identify.

Tim did not hesitate to identify Christy as the person who emerged from inside the queen's float. Her wedding ring, larger than normal, sparkled in the morning sun leading Tim to think the ring was bigger than it really was.

❀❀❀

Lou and Jack would testify when the accused went to trial. Detective Morrison wrapped up the case with Lou and Jack's blessing. Sara and her mom came back to Traverse City from Northport with a new bond, one they will never lose.

THE END

EPILOGUE

Christy Johnson and **Steve Tuttle** were convicted of the murder of Tom McNutt. They were also convicted of the kidnapping and attempted murder of Sara Laskey, and also found guilty of the attempted murder of Lou Searing. They were sentenced to life in prison with no chance for parole. At the trial it was revealed that Christy had embezzled several million dollars to feed her gambling addiction and to cover her many losses.

Joanne Tuttle was found guilty of aiding and abetting the murder of Tom McNutt and the attempted murder of Lou Searing. She was sentenced to twenty years in a women's correctional facility in northern Michigan.

Stone Elliott left the Traverse City area and now lives in Phoenix, Arizona. He has no regrets about turning against those who killed Tom and planned to kill Lou.

Eric Williams had nothing to do with the crimes. He is now the leading candidate for Grand Marshal of next year's Cherry Festival Parade.

Lou Searing and **Jack Kelly** were given keys to Traverse City for their work in helping solve the murder of Tom McNutt. A long article about them appeared in the *Record Eagle* newspaper.

The **Traverse City Police** have no suspects in the Northernmost Winery bombing but are fairly certain the fire was set by someone to whom Christy owed a huge gambling debt.

Police **Chief Stacy Bixler** became Police Chief in Bay City. It pays more and gives her a new challenge in law enforcement. **Detective Rod Morrison** was appointed Chief of Police, a much deserved promotion.

Chief Bixler reimbursed **Zeb Horvath** for the destroyed mannequin and an inexpensive sport coat.

Jerry Waters continues to serve as Festival Director. The festival enjoyed a record year in terms of visitors and expected economic bonuses for the community.

The **Northernmost Winery** was sold to the son of a winery owner in Berrien Springs in southwest Michigan. He had a good reputation and would run a profitable winery.

Sara Laskey and **Tim Jacobs** were considered heroes by the Traverse City community. Sara is receiving therapy for the trauma she suffered in her kidnapping, and she is expected to adjust well.

Ethel Albers eventually regained her sight through much counseling and therapy. She and Herm found her disease fascinating and enjoyed reviewing her collection of 'sightings.'

Heather Adams became the brew master at a winery in Wisconsin. The same winery also hired **Dennis Smith** and **Anthony Kellogg.** All three received much higher salaries.

Corky retired after failing to meet his quota of selling wine corks for the first time in 41 years.

Carol recovered completely from her premonition of Lou's impending doom. It was a scary experience for her; she fully expected it to happen as she "saw" it in her mind.

Lou and Carol did not purchase a home in Manistee. They decided they loved Grand Haven, their church, and their neighbors. And living near Lou's sister, Gayle, was important to them also.

Lou spent the rest of the summer writing, and enjoying walks on the beach with **Carol** and **Samm.**

A TRIBUTE TO
WESTON BALDWIN

If ever an engineer's career was practically certain after the first five years of life, it could belong to Weston Baldwin. He bonded with Legos at three and four years of age. His detailed and intricate structures are conversation pieces.

Weston contemplates a large assortment of Legos and spends hours building whatever fills his imagination at the time. He even built his own version of the popular television show, *Wipeout.*

But who can tell what career choices await young Weston? If he ends up an engineer, the credit must go to the family and relatives who provided him with a substantial arsenal of Legos.

*To order additional copies of this book,
or any others written by Richard L. Baldwin,
please go to buttonwoodpress.com*